THE CHRISTMAS CAT FROM HELL

D.W. HITZ

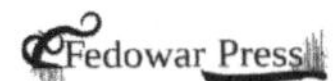

Fedowar Press, LLC

ALSO BY D.W. HITZ

Judith's Prophecy (Big Sky Terror Book 1)
Judith's Blood (Big Sky Terror Book 2)
Judith's Fall (Big Sky Terror Book 3)
Gods are Born
Brady: A Novella
Bloodtooth
Our Trip Through Hell
Garrets Lodge
Food Court of the Damned
Black Creek Mystic
The Shadow Over Lone Wolf Lake
The Christmas Cat From Hell

Stay up to date with D.W. by becoming a member at
patreon.com/dwhitz

THE CHRISTMAS CAT FROM HELL

D.W. HITZ

DECEMBER 13TH

12 Days 'til Christmas.

BLINDING PAIN CLAWED ITS way into Julie's left ear and quickly faded into a freezing burn as the snowball crumbled into her hair and trickled down her face. Crystals scattered away across her parka, though more than she liked snuck into the gap between her bright-pink scarf and her neck, giving her shivers that would only slow her down—if she let them.

While Julie realized at that second that she should have listened to her mother and tucked her scarf into her jacket a bit tighter, the oncoming flash of cold tingling across her skin, she was more focused on the dive into her team's base. She slid across the snowy path on her belly and stopped two feet shy of the entrance.

"I got her!" Tommy Higgins shouted. The thirteen-year-old was too smug for his own good, and at that moment, Julie really hated the sound of his voice.

"Keep throwing!" Julie's brother Simon screamed at his teammate. "Don't let them fire back." Both boys had fortified themselves behind the family's backyard picnic table with their stack of snowballs, and if there was anything in the world the twelve-year-old sibling looked forward to all year long, it was tagging his little sister as many times as possible with snowballs without consequences.

He threw the projectile in his hand as Julie rose. It hit her in the thigh as she scurried into the girls' base.

"Come on!" Marcy screamed from inside the geodesic dome the girls—or *Team Pink* as they called themselves—were using as their base. Before the snow started in November, Julie and Simon had wrapped the thing in a big blue tarp, and now it looked more like a four-foot-tall igloo than a backyard jungle gym.

Marcy held a snowy round in her hand, bobbing her head side to side, trying to judge what would be her best shot at the boys.

Julie climbed through the opening, snagged a new snowball from Team Pink's pile, and took aim. She didn't weigh her options more than what she could calculate in that split second. The way she saw it, they needed to blind the boys with an onslaught of raw power, not precision. She let loose her volley and pulled her hand back into their base just in time to slip out of the way of Tommy's next shot.

She watched her white ball soar through the air, through the gap between the igloo and the picnic table, and slam right into her target. She no longer felt the burning in her ear as she saw her missile slam into Tommy's nose and explode. Her satisfaction was the best painkiller.

"Agh!" Tommy screamed, and cowered behind cover.

Marcy threw another round at Simon, and it went flying over his head. He fired back, and it exploded on the rim of the igloo's opening, showering the girls in crystals but doing no real damage.

"Together," Julie commanded, and she and Marcy both armed themselves. They aimed at the picnic table, and Julie said, "Ready?" She waited for what she knew was coming.

A red-faced Tommy stood, baring teeth and wide eyes. He was raising his arm, hoping for intense retaliation, and Julie saw his glowing nose and imagined Rudolf's—a great big red target.

"Now!" she shouted.

Team Pink let loose.

Snowballs flew.

They pulled back inside the igloo but not before Julie watched Tommy's shot slip past her head and her own smash into the boy's nose and explode for the second time in their neighborhood war.

"Shit!" Tommy turned and stood. He started walking toward the front yard, toward his house across the street.

"Tom?" Simon brushed snow from the top of his head, his own wound from the girls' attack. "Where're you going?"

"Uh—I'm hungry. I'm going to eat something," Tommy snapped.

"We're playing!" Simon raised his hands into the air. "Aren't we gonna storm their base?"

"Maybe later. Hungry." Tommy was at the side of the house and turned back. His nose was indeed glowing as bright as a magical reindeer's after that second hit. "Let's play video games."

Simon huffed. "Okay." He stood and followed his friend.

"We win!" Marcy yelled.

"No!" Simon argued. "We're not done. Just taking a break."

"We win," Julie repeated.

"No!" Simon kept walking. "Just a break!"

"We totally won." Julie grinned at Marcy. She sat in the igloo, completely satisfied with herself, unaware of what was happening inside her house. She only had another hour at most to play in the snow with sunset coming around five—she couldn't concern herself with what Mom and Dad were up to when playtime was so limited.

Still, she felt two things. There was a warmth, almost like something was in her lap and heating her, a warmth like a furry electric blanket that was just for her. The second thing she felt was a tingling apprehension—she wasn't sure exactly what or who was the cause, but there was a danger coming. It was a danger where she couldn't tell the source or the target, but it was coming as surely as Christmas was on its way.

She brushed those feelings aside as she spotted her sled leaning on the side of the house. There was no time for worry in the waning winter daylight. There was still fun to be had today.

When Julie went inside, the living room's wood stove was lit, and she could hear Mom doing something in the kitchen. It took Julie pulling off her gloves and snow boots for her to feel just how much the cold had crept into her body. Her toes were nearly numb, and her skin was freezing to the touch after shedding her coat and hanging it on the rack.

She shuffled across the carpet and held her hands up to the fire, hoping for a quick thaw. She rubbed her palms together as she peeked through the doorway into the kitchen, wondering what Mom was up to.

"Mom?" she called, and immediately knew she wasn't loud enough. The blower in the wood stove was going, and Mom's Bluetooth speaker was on in the kitchen—Leo Sayer proclaimed his love the way only 1970's vocalists could. Julie called again. "Mom?"

The living room sparkled from not just the flickering fire but also the lights on the tree, the Christmas lights trimming the room and running around the windows, the silver garland festooned between banister posts, and various battery-powered miniature porcelain figurines. It smelled of pine and cinnamon, and even through the blower, the fire, the music, and the radio, Julie could hear her mother singing in the kitchen. It may not have been a carol, but she heard her mother's tone and spirit, and that spirit lifted her up.

The Butlers weren't very well off, even for the modest neighborhood they resided in, south of the railroad tracks on the eastern side of Custer Falls. The things they owned were cared for like they could never be replaced because it was likely that if broken, they wouldn't have been, not with Mom's retail income and Dad's limited few hours a week that his nerve-damaged legs allowed him to work. They wouldn't have had the house at all if it hadn't been passed down to Mom from her aunt before Julie was born. They didn't call themselves poor, but they knew they were at the bottom of the hill when it came to most of the town—and Mom refused to let any of that stop them from filling their house with love.

In the week that led up to Thanksgiving, Mom was pulling the decorations out of the garage. While so many people were out shopping on Black Friday, Mom was hanging garland and humming the songs that would fill the air for the next month. By the time December started, Julie, Simon, Mom, and Dad would be watching Christmas movies each night and laughing and planning for every bit of winter fun they could include.

It was infectious the way Mom filled the house and the family with her spirit, and it made Julie unable to stop herself from grinning when she was in the presence of it all.

Her fingers toasty and the front of her legs almost burning from standing so close to the stove, Julie headed toward the kitchen. It had to be dinner; that was what Mom was working on, she was sure. Though maybe it was a treat? Cookies for the neighbors, or a pie—she wouldn't mind licking the mixing bowls, but she didn't want to carry any cookies to Tommy Higgins's house—Simon could do that.

Julie tilted her head, looking at the stove as she passed through the kitchen doorway. Mom wasn't there, and a cold feeling of trepidation shot down her spine. She looked the other way, toward the table, and there Mom was.

That cold trepidation throbbed.

She didn't know of Mom ever doing anything nefarious, either that day or any day in the past, but for some reason, at that moment, she couldn't help but feel like Mom was up to something that she should not have been doing.

Her mother stood at the kitchen table, her back to Julie. Whatever she was up to on that table crinkled and skidded like paper crunching and sliding on cardboard.

"Mom?" This time, Julie was sure to speak louder than Mom's Bluetooth speaker on the counter.

Mom jumped and spun, her arms up and her eyes wide as she tried to block Julie's view of the table. "Julie!"

The crinkling noises continued behind Mom, and Julie squinted, a sour feeling inside her stomach as she tried to see around her mother. "What is that?"

Mom frowned and dropped her arms. The crinkling turned to scratching.

"Mom?"

"Fine." Mom huffed and then smiled. "I guess I can't really make you wait for Christmas for this one, but I was hoping to build up a little suspense before you got it."

"What are you talking about?"

Mom rolled her eyes. She was nearly bursting. "Close your eyes."

"Okay..." Julie did as she was told. She heard little other than the same shuffling of paper, though it was coming closer. It made her heart race.

"Okay," Mom said, "open them."

When she opened her eyelids, Julie met the gaze of a pair of wide, black and golden eyes, the shiniest and cutest little eyes she had ever seen. She couldn't help smiling as her shivers slipped away, and the furry little face of a tan tabby kitten with dark-brown markings stared and opened its whiskered mouth in a high-pitched *hello* meow.

He sat in Mom's red-wrapping-lined box. His ears were too big for his head, and his paws kneaded the air as they reached for her. He looked into her eyes, and she felt warmth overwhelm her the way only real love could. He wanted to knead and cuddle her, and she wanted to stroke him and care for him forever. He was the thing she had been wanting most, the thing that had been missing from her life, and every drop of hesitation and dread drained from her body as she reached for him.

She was crying when her hands slipped under his furry armpits and took him. His loud little purr vibrated her fingers as she pulled him to her chest, and she instantly knew they would be friends forever. She even knew his name: Jynx.

<hr>

Derek Polson stepped into the night from his front door, a bag of garbage in one hand while holding his jacket tight over his chest with the other. The wind whipped across his face, burning his nose and reminding him that midnight was the worst time to take out the trash. He would have left the tied-up bag next to the can in the kitchen if he thought Matty, his dachshund, wouldn't dig into it and leave slimy meat wrappers and empty dog food cans sprawled across the kitchen floor by morning.

He had just closed the door when Matty started barking. The dog did that when he was left behind, part separation anxiety and part disdain for not leading the trip, wherever it was to, though this time the pitch was a little shriller, a little more anxious than usual.

"Shut up," Derek snapped through the door. "I'll be right back." Every time the pup did this since winter started, he was reminded that Matty would rather be inside, even if the dog forgot over and over again—Matty hated when the snow touched his belly, which was almost instantly after an inch stuck to the grass. Besides, it was the dog's fault that he had to do this. *Let him bark.*

He shivered and started down the steps.

There was a smell on the wind as he walked the sidewalk and passed the garage. It was a deep kind of animal musk, a wild smell that he may have imagined belonged to a bear or a wolf. It was a heavy scent, one he would have never expected in his neighborhood, and he guessed it was coming from the Butlers' house. They lived just next door, beyond the gap after his garage, and that woman, Erica, was always up to something strange—her and her kids.

He turned the corner and could barely see the garbage cans on the side of his house. Usually, the motion sensors on the floodlight would catch him the moment he rounded that corner, but for some reason, the darkness prevailed.

Whatever. He could see well enough in the dark winter night to drop the bag in the can. He would figure out the floodlight failure tomorrow.

The stench was worse the closer he came to the trash. It was thick in the freezing air, in a way that cold air wasn't right to hold. It was a moist, rancid odor that should have needed humidity to contain it, but there it was, this godawful smell, soaking into Derek's nose like he was a sponge and that odor was just waiting for him.

It sent a cold spike down his limbs, stiffer than the freezing air, giving him a sensation like he was wearing nothing at all in some arctic plain. His stomach rose into his chest, and his fingers trembled. He imagined something massive and deadly somewhere ahead—it was an instinctual fear that gripped him in a way that he would have said only animals felt—he was a rabbit on that frigid plain as some hungry predator lay in wait, ready to ambush him at any second.

There was something in that darkness ahead. He didn't know how he knew it, but he knew it, and even as his rational mind begged him to calm down from his frontal lobe, his soul knew better. He needed to get the hell out of there. He needed to run, no matter how silly he might feel tomorrow for letting little things like a smell and the darkness of night get to him.

The snow crunched.

He couldn't see where it came from. It was behind the trash cans. It was toward the Butlers' house. It was on his roof. It was everywhere. It was nowhere, hiding somehow in his mind.

"Hello?" He uttered a weak word, a word he prayed would be answered with a kind voice while knowing there was no chance.

The snow crunched once more.

The bag slipped from Derek's hand as he spun and dug his feet into the ground to sprint toward his front door.

He didn't make it out of the darkness. He didn't see what took him. He only felt the sharp stinging pain as something dug into his back so hard and so fast that he couldn't even scream.

December 14th

11 Days 'til Christmas.

J ULIE FOUND HER FATHER in the living room when she came downstairs with Jynx in hand. Dad was in his recliner, having his usual Sunday morning bowl of oatmeal and blueberries while watching one of those shows where men went into the woods in search of Bigfoot. Julie didn't understand the draw—they never found him—but it was Dad's thing.

She sat on the couch and yawned. Jynx stood and stretched in her lap, then yawned as well. She hoped her new boy had a good night's sleep. He was cuddled beside her for most of the night, so she supposed he had.

He half climbed up her chest with his front paws and patted at her face. He let out the smallest meow, and she couldn't help but smile and squint at his overwhelming cuteness.

"Oh my god, you must be a starving, little guy."

Dad turned in his chair, examining both her and the cat. "How are you two getting along?" He winced, and Julie knew his nerves must be acting up.

"Wonderful." Julie stood. She rubbed Dad's shoulder and gave him a one-armed hug. She wished she could do more for him. "Come on, Jynxie, let's get you some breakfast."

Dad nodded and turned back to his show. She carried her boy to the kitchen with breakfast on her mind.

Mom was doing her baking and humming along to the Rat Pack

singing Christmas classics. The kitchen air was thick with the smell of cookies, and Julie debated stealing a few, wondering if she could get away with it. They were just resting on the wire rack on the counter, the golden-white hue of perfectly baked sugar cookies teasing her.

With another meow from her new child, she ultimately decided against the theft. She would get a cookie later, one way or the other. Cereal was good for the moment.

She grabbed a small plate and took a can of kitten food from the pile on the counter that Mom had revealed the previous night. She set Jynx, the plate, and the can on the table, then popped the top and attempted to shake the can's contents onto the dish. The food didn't drop free, and this time, when Jynx cried—the smell of fish and seafood medley heavy in the air—he was louder and distinctly more insistent.

"Okay, okay." She left the table, and he meowed again, and again, somehow deeper, once she had a butter knife in hand on the way back. "Jeez, Jynxie, it's comin'."

She failed to notice her mother had turned and was watching the scene with curiosity.

Julie scraped the can empty onto the plate, nearly smacking Jynx with the falling food. The cat couldn't wait for her to finish and was eating the raining meaty morsels the second the food touched the ceramic.

"That's how babies are," Mom said.

"What?" Julie spun and locked eyes with her smirking mother.

"They want what they want, and they want it *now*."

"Are you implying *I'm* like that?"

"Not at all." She shook her head, smirk still glued to her lips, then she turned back to her mixing bowl.

"I'm not like that," Julie said under her breath.

She ate her cereal from the box, ignoring the weird meat/cat food smell, and watched Jynx finish, lick the plate, then clean his paws one toe at a time.

She thought for a second that he looked larger than he did last night, but he couldn't have grown overnight—right?

Julie heard the repeated thud of her brother coming down the stairs and imagined having another snowball fight today. It would be nice to see Tommy's nose glow red again. But she had promised Marcy they would play at her house, or maybe catch up on some sledding they were behind on—the snow was late to fall this winter.

Marcy could change her mind, though, once she hears about Jynx.

When Simon entered the kitchen, Jynx stopped what he was doing and eyed Julie's brother. It was the type of look that Julie imagined a cat might give to a mouse or something it was thinking of pouncing on. She wasn't sure why he was doing that. Jynx and Simon had met last night, and she thought it had gone well.

Simon looked at the cat and rolled his eyes. "We're letting that thing on the table now?"

Julie couldn't help but squint as she stared down her brother. "We let you in the house, don't we?"

He squinted back. "Well, I guess we already let a dog in."

"Stop it, you two," Mom scolded. "Both of you, be nice." She went back to humming along with Bing Crosby.

Mom's command didn't stop his glare as he walked to the pantry to look for his own breakfast, or Julie's as she followed him with her eyes. Jynx, though, he set his head on his leg, staring off into the living room, as if the small cat had more important things to ponder, as if he was looking past the front wall of the house into the neighborhood beyond.

Adam Milton watched from his front window as the Butler girl and the Burrows girl carried their sleds up the street toward the hilltop intersection. It was the stupidest thing he had ever seen—or so he told himself, since he had done quite similar things in his days of youthful ignorance, though he would never admit to them. His youth was long gone, lost more than half a century ago, and though it wasn't always clear to him, there were good reasons why those days were better off not remembered.

He watched the neighborhood kids do this same thing every year, and every year, he thought to himself how dumb it was. As soon as there was an inch of snow on the ground, they would climb the road to the intersection of 35th Avenue and Railroad Street, place their sleds in the middle of the goddamn road, and off they went down the middle of the asphalt, like they were a goddamn car—like they were indestructible. They went one after the other, flying down the middle of the road without a care in the world or fear of traffic, then up the hill to do it again.

Sometimes there would be as many as ten of them doing the same moronic thing.

Adam coughed. He coughed so hard and so deep he saw spots in his vision as he tasted the salty (and somewhat bloody) slime coming up from his lungs. He grasped the edge of the end table for balance, knowing that if the oncoming lightheadedness ended up being enough for him to pass out, that little table wasn't going to help at all.

The kids walked out of view, and he backed up and sat in his chair, wiping the sweat from his forehead and bracing himself for the next wave of coughing he sensed was coming. His lungs closed in, swelling around the clumps of phlegm, and air, saliva, and mucus shot from his mouth as he raced to cover his lips. Cough after cough, his lungs tightened and his chest burned. The room felt dimmer, and the air he was able to pull in between belts of hacking shrank.

Adam grabbed his tea and guzzled it, hoping it would coat his throat just enough, when another round of coughing forced its way through.

By the time his lungs let him take a break, the room was spinning and his entire chest was in pain. He sat with his head back in his chair and heard the idiot neighbor kids shriek as they slid down the road with only the Almighty holding back the vehicles that would otherwise turn them into roadkill.

A phrase came to mind which he muttered under his weak breath: "God watches over children and fools."

He hoped they would get hit—just for a moment, just because they needed to be taught a lesson. He hoped God would slip up and let some random pizza delivery boy race down the hill and take one of them out to teach the rest.

It was bad to think that way; he knew it was wicked. But with his head and lungs and half his body seeming to be falling apart, it gave him a small bit of needed satisfaction.

He peeked out the window from his chair, and something small and furry tore across the Butlers' lawn. It was probably a squirrel. He didn't give it another thought.

He didn't notice the cat sneaking into the broken filter on the side of his house that allowed his dryer to vent.

Julie's sled slowed in front of Marcy's house, and she put her feet down, one on each side of the plastic dream-ride. Marcy stopped beside her, and together, they watched a police cruiser pull in front of them and then into the Polsons' driveway—the one right after Julie's.

She got as shiver as she watched an officer get out of the car, look up and down the street, settling his gaze on her. It wasn't that Julie was doing anything wrong—she was pretty sure she wasn't breaking any laws (that she knew of)—it was more of a feeling that something was wrong and that officer was there to deal with it.

But what could have been wrong? Custer Falls was a pretty safe place. Maybe it wasn't in the past—she had heard stories of crazy stuff that happened years ago—but it was a safe, small town, according to Mom.

That officer, though. He looked at Julie like he was worried about her—like there was some imminent threat nearby—and she could feel that worry inside. It wasn't just in that cop. It was hanging in the air like an ornament on a tree, ready to be smacked off by a runaway pet. There was a danger in her neighborhood even if she couldn't see it, even if Mom said this place was safe.

The officer broke eye contact and walked up the Polsons' driveway.

"Why do you think he's here?" Marcy asked.

Before the policeman made it to the steps, Kelly Polson, the woman of the house, opened the door. Her eyes were red, and she held a tissue up to her nose.

"I don't know, but she looks upset," Julie said.

"Yeah."

Mrs. Polson held open the door, welcoming the officer inside though Julie could tell from the serious looks on both of their faces that it was not a social call. Something was wrong at that house—was that what she was feeling?

"I don't like it," Julie said.

"Whatever." Marcy was back on her feet with her sled in hand. She wasn't one to dwell on things that didn't concern her. Julie admired that about her friend, the way she could just drop things that didn't matter and move on. "Let's do another run."

Up the hill they went, then down again. Harvey and Lee from the other side of the hill joined them, and they raced, only crashing into parked cars on the sides of the road once or twice. Around the time that Simon and Tommy joined them at the top of the run, Julie felt her stomach rumbling, so instead of sledding with them, the girls headed to Marcy's house for a snack.

They almost made it to Marcy's door when the Custer Falls police officer emerged from the Polsons' house looking a bit frustrated. Mrs. Polson's eyes were even redder, and her cheeks matched in brightness as their wet skin glistened in the early afternoon sun.

Julie and Marcy were captivated by the sight—Julie wasn't quite sure why. They watched Kelly Polson weep, and when the officer caught them staring, he shouted.

"You kids stay out of the road! You want to get hit by a car?" The man seemed rather flustered, more so than Julie imagined a cop should have been.

What had happened in there? And where was Mr. Polson?

The cop grumbled and glared up the hill, where Harvey, Lee, Simon, and Tommy had all stopped getting ready for their next trip down and were instead watching the cop. The officer shook his head and got in his car like there was no use in whatever he had been mulling over.

"What was all that about?" Marcy wondered. She didn't wait for an answer, and by the time the police car was out of the driveway and turning off 35th, she was at her door and waiting for Julie. "You coming or what?"

Julie nodded and followed.

Julie did not like that Marcy's mother smoked cigarettes. Their house always held what she imagined was an ashy smell—she didn't know what else to compare it to—and it made her feel like anything she touched in the house was going to make her fingers come away with ash on them. But that didn't happen because Lisa Burrows was an impeccably clean woman, barely allowing the ash from a single cigarette to settle before emptying the tray into the trash. And the fact was, she only smoked in a single room, her bedroom, but that didn't stop Julie, who didn't know any better, from assuming the whole place was some sort of smoker's club.

In Marcy's kitchen, Julie and Marcy sat at the table. That was how it was at Marcy's. Within a minute, Ms. Burrows was there like a waitress to take their orders. The only thing missing was a pad of paper and a pen.

Marcy ordered a grilled cheese, and Julie said she would have the same thing. She didn't really like grilled cheeses that much, but she didn't want to be rude and figured it would be rude if she made Marcy's mom cook two different things. Ms. Burrows would have done it—Julie knew that—and she wouldn't have complained a bit, but Julie would have still felt bad.

As the smell of buttery, cheesy toast filled the kitchen, Marcy talked without barely a break to inhale about her upcoming piano recital, and how hard her new songs were, and that Julie just had to come to this one and hear it all. In fact, Julie had heard each song about a thousand times through the walls from her house, but she nodded and agreed to attend the recital as she dissected each item on the Burrows' walls.

There were dozens of pieces of sheet music and pictures of Marcy over the years. There were little trophies from soccer and ribbons from awards at school. Pictures of someone older—maybe Marcy's grandmother—hung, and there were things Julie didn't recognize (old pottery, maybe?) that decorated the top of one of the cabinets. It was all quite neat and organized, but there was something off about it all, something that had always bugged Julie, and she was just now understanding—there was not a single image of a man in the entire house.

At Julie's house, they had family photos, some of her dad in his bachelor days. There were pictures of Simon, pictures of their cousins, some boys, pictures of their grandparents, including both grandfathers though she had never met her mother's father. But she didn't think she had ever seen a single thing—either image or item—that resembled a male in Marcy's house.

She opened her mouth to ask about it when Ms. Burrows set their plates on the table. Each held a grilled cheese sandwich, sliced in half, with a pile of fish-shaped crackers between the halves. Something told Julie to take a bite and think first before asking.

Ms. Burrows made hot cocoa while they ate. Julie found her mind drift away from the silly question of men in the Burrows' house to wondering how Jynx was doing. He was a little guy, and he might have been lonely in her room with her gone and playing all day. Maybe they should head to her house and pet him for a bit before sledding more.

They finished their sandwiches and drank their cocoa, and Julie had the strangest feeling that while she had wondered about Jynx, he was actually in the house with them. It was dumb, but it felt like he was as at home in her neighborhood as she was, that he was, in fact, all over it, like she was.

But that was silly.

They left for the Butlers' to shower her boy with scratches, and she decided she could ask Marcy all the weird questions she had some other time.

As Adam Milton walked from his kitchen to his living room, clutching his chest and hoping not to face another round of coughing until he was seated, he couldn't help but think there was something a bit misplaced in his house. It hit him what it was as he neared his seat. There was a smell like an animal, lingering in the air, a smell he had not been in the presence of in a very long time.

His heart instantly raced, and his chest tightened.

The tickle in his old, sore throat took hold, and he collapsed into his seat, coughing uncontrollably, the room shaking all around him. The light dipped and swelled as he moved and tried to catch his breath. The scent grew thicker as the thing he hoped to never see again moved closer from the shadow in the corner of the room. It grew larger with each gasp for air, more real with each strain on his lungs.

But it couldn't have been. It just couldn't.

Its eyes were huge, black, and glassy, and they reflected his pale, suffocating face. Its fur was deep and dark, like what was inside it, a mix of blacks and reddish dark browns that hid the blood it took from those it punished. Its breath was a wall of hot, damp hunger that soaked him as he pressed himself backward into his seat, hoping to get himself together, hoping he would gain control of his body and get a chance to run.

That was a stupid concern. He knew if it wanted him there was nowhere to run. There was no speed he could accelerate to that it could not top. He was at its mercy.

He leaned over the arm of his chair, his breath failing and his sight filling with spots. His mind went to his grandmother, to the warnings she gave him.

He was only a boy then, but he remembered, her voice ringing clearly in his mind as it had that day: *In the old country, they knew. Those who mistreated the children would pay.*

He remembered the bloody houses and streets as it sniffed him. He had tried to block it out, to think of that week as some bad dream that had happened to a child he no longer was, a dream that should have been forgotten. It huffed on his ear as he fought for air.

But how could someone forget that week?

DECEMBER 15TH

10 Days 'til Christmas.

THERE WAS ALWAYS A lot of screaming in the cafeteria of Custer Falls Elementary when the bell to end fourth period rang and the hall filled with children, but with Christmas and, maybe even more importantly, winter break just a few days away, there was an extra buzz of excitement in the air.

Microwaves whirred into action, heating up lunches kids brought from home. Cafeteria workers handed out servings of hamburgers, pizza, and à la carte snacks that the managing company overcharged parents for. Teachers hovered on the edges of the room. Together, it would have looked like a normal day, but each student knew differently. They knew it was a countdown to Christmas, and less than two weeks held them back from the magic of presents and vacation and candy, a break in the monotony of school-home-school-home, and an embrace of freedom and winter fun.

Julie stood in line for the microwave on the west side of the room, away from the pizza line and closer to the recess exit. She didn't have anything to cook; her lunch was in her backpack, a combination of a cold-cut sandwich and a loose piece of fruit or two. She was holding the spot for Marcy, whose mother sent her with things to cook daily, and Marcy, being a year younger, was in fourth grade, not fifth, and for some reason, that meant she got released to lunch five minutes later than Julie.

It was a daily occurrence, waiting for Marcy, and while Julie usually didn't mind, today she was itching for Marcy to hurry up and get there. It may have been the heightened volume in the room, or it may have been Julie's urge to get home and check on Jynx—he was so loving and playful that morning that she hadn't really wanted to leave him—but it also had to do with the news that she had won her Home Room Winter Raffle, and in her backpack was a bundle of candy that she could in no way finish all by herself.

The microwave dinged, and Marty Fox walked away with his plastic bowl of cheesy noodles. It meant it was Julie's (or Marcy's) turn, but Julie had nothing to stick inside it, and the line behind her was hungry and waiting. She was about to tell Joey Morris to go ahead when Marcy seemed to appear out of the blue.

Marcy was bubbling, her eyes bright and the grin across her face all-consuming. She grabbed Julie and pulled her from the line with both hands, ignoring the fact that she would have to get in the back to cook anything, and that would take half of their lunch period. If she realized that, it didn't show because she wasn't unpacking her lunch bag or anything.

"Marcy?" Julie pointed at the line.

"It's fine." She pulled Julie toward their regular table near the door. "You won't believe it." She squealed and ushered them both into their usual seats at the end of the table.

"What? What?" Julie couldn't imagine that whatever news Marcy had was better than her giant bag of free candy, but she needed to know.

Marcy gazed around, cautious of who was listening, then she started. "You know how Katelyn's cousin Josh was being questioned by the police when the pastor from his youth group called and said his gun was missing?"

"Yeah—didn't they search Josh's house and everything trying to find it?"

"Yeah, and they never did—so all the kids in math were like 'I'm not going to the Friday show'—oh, that's a thing, we're all going to the movies on Friday, and you have to come, I'll get your ticket if you need me to—but they're all acting like Josh is just going to show up and start mass shooting the theater or something. I was going to tell them to shut up, that was dumb—I mean, why would he do that, just because he has a gun?—but then Ben kind of stepped next to me and was like, 'You need to go,' and, 'I'll make sure you're okay.'"

"Ben Andrews? The one with the short, brown hair and the—"

"And the eyes that melt your soul? Yes! I could barely breathe. I didn't know what to say. Thankfully, Katelyn snapped at everyone that her cousin was innocent," Marcy rolled her eyes, "like, really? But either way, it shut everyone up, and then Mrs. Fincher made us all be quiet and work on *in-class homework...*"

"Well? Was that it?"

"No..." Marcy pulled a piece of paper from her pocket, glanced around again, double-checking that no one was watching, and she unfolded it. "Look."

Scrawled in almost illegible handwriting was the message: *Will you sit with me at the movie?* There was also a box with *yes* beside it and a box with *no.*

Julie's jaw dropped. "From Ben?"

Marcy nodded. "He slipped it in my hand as we left math and told me to give it back in English."

"What are you going to do?"

"Say *yes!*"

They both hopped up and down in their seats.

Julie was so happy for her friend. She reached into her bag. "I have the perfect celebration treat for this." She set her lunch on the table to Marcy's tilted stare. "Hold on." She dug deeper and pulled out the grocery bag full of sugar.

"What is that?" Marcy's eyes were nearly as big as they had been when entering the cafeteria.

"I won the raffle—the one where everyone donated Halloween candy and got five points of extra credit. It's all mine!" Julie spread the bag wide so they could both see inside.

"Yes!" Marcy's hand hovered over the top as she zeroed in on what she wanted. She snagged a Cherry Chew and unwrapped it. "The perfect celebration candy."

Julie scanned the bag and spotted a sour jawbreaker. If she was going to skip lunch, she might as well grab something that would last the whole period. She unwrapped it and popped it into her mouth, and the conversation shifted to ideas of how Marcy should deliver the note back to her crush, then what she might wear, then other activities that could precede or follow the movie. They failed to finish the conversation before lunch was over and the bell rang, and the cafeteria started clearing out with everyone heading to after-lunch recess.

They packed up their things, aiming for the exit, both smiling and imagining the fun to come as winter break started on Friday, when something snagged Julie's foot.

She thought she had passed the table before stepping, but it was hard to say for sure when neck deep in conversation with Marcy. She must have caught the edge of her shoe on the table's leg, because whether she thought it should have happened or not, she was going down, tripping, her arms full of backpack, the floor rising toward her face.

Julie's response, based on pure instinct, was to let go of her backpack and land palms-down on the floor. It stopped her from falling, and had the backpack not been between her and the solid ground, it may have been the perfect choice. Unfortunately, the backpack was there.

Her chest and face slammed down into the book-filled canvas bag. Her chin hit a particularly stiff section, likely the binding of her math book, and her jaw clacked upward, banging into her jawbreaker, slamming the candy into her upper teeth.

There was a crack and a rush of pain before Julie understood what had happened. Tears flowing, she moved her tongue in search of the source of her new agony. She found both the jawbreaker and half of a tooth floating in her saliva.

Despite the year difference in their ages, Simon and Tommy were both in the seventh grade at Custer Falls Middle School. Tommy had been held back in the fourth grade when a fight on the playground left him hospitalized for two months and he never caught back up. While they would have liked to have been in all the same classes together, they were actually only in one: PE, during last period.

A lot of schools up in the Northwest, Simon was pretty sure, would have brought their kids inside on blustery winter days. Not CFMS or, at least, not Coach Cobbuge—or Coach Cabbage, as they called him. Cabbage seemed like a sadist to Simon. He wanted the class in the baking sun on late May days and in the freezing cold in the middle of winter. While the other PE teachers brought their classes into the gym on those occasions, Cabbage seemed to get a thrill from saying, "No, it'll be good for you to be outside."

So today, on the ten-degree, snow-covered soccer practice field, with a ten-mile-per-hour wind cutting across the class, Simon and his fellow students played some variant of kickball.

Some of the kids did, anyway. Most of them just stood and let the ball roll past as they tightened their jackets to their waists and kept their faces pointed away from the wind.

"Come on, guys!" Cabbage yelled. "Get moving! It'll keep you warm."

He acted like he meant it, but Simon could see a glimmer in the coach's eyes, a little upturn of the corner of his mouth—the man was enjoying making the kids freeze, no matter how he may have tried to hide it.

"Sick prick," Tommy muttered just loud enough for Simon to hear.

"He gets off on it," Simon muttered back.

Neither of them was playing the game other than offering a fake attempt here or there when the ball rolled by, lifting a leg outward ever so slightly.

"He wants us to suffer," Tommy said.

"Someone should force him to be out in the cold without a choice."

"Yeah," Tommy agreed.

"Kick it!" Cabbage shouted at Robin Andrews, who just stared at him as the ball rolled past.

Simon chuckled. Catching sight of who the coach was yelling at reminded him, "Weren't you going to ask Robin to the movies?"

"Ugh," Tommy grunted. "Yeah, so what?"

"Well, did you?"

Tommy kind of leaned away and came back, a groan under his breath. "I was going to."

"Well, go do it."

Tommy looked around, noting the coach, who had followed the ball downfield, then the other kids in their various bunches.

"Eh, okay." Tommy started across the fifteen feet that separated them from Robin.

Simon had to stop his mouth from dropping open. Yeah, he had practically dared Tommy to do it, but the fact that his friend actually was—it was stunning.

Tommy stopped beside Robin. He didn't look at her; he half watched

Cabbage and half stared at the ball, but he started talking.

She turned to him. She had to raise her head a little, and either that or what he was saying made her crack a smile—most of the boys in seventh were shorter than the girls, and Tommy was probably the tallest boy in the grade.

He still didn't look at her, but he finished talking, and she nodded. She said something, and he turned away and headed back toward Simon without uttering anything in response.

"Ball!" Cabbage screamed, and the round, rubber sphere came whizzing across the showy grass.

Simon lifted his foot in a feigned attempt to kick it and let it roll on by.

Tommy stood next to Simon, and they both ignored the kids twenty feet behind them, tracking down the ball and sending it back forward.

"Well?" Simon insisted. "What did she say?"

"Yes," he muttered.

Tommy was trying to play it cool, but Simon could see the grin inside peeking just barely through.

They were both looking ahead, not really watching Robin but keeping her in sight, and she turned and glanced at Tommy before turning back toward the coach.

"Dog," Simon whispered.

"What can I say? I got skills."

"Shut up."

"Now you ask someone."

"What?" It hadn't occurred to Simon that he might have to do it too. "Why—who?"

"I'm not going on this date alone." He gestured vaguely across the field. "Someone, but someone fun. Don't ask anyone bitchy."

"Yeah. Okay..." He thought about it for a moment. "I'll ask tomorrow."

"Man, I just asked. You gotta do it now."

"She's not here."

There was a moment of silence as Tommy thought and Simon refused to say any more.

"Oh." Tommy swayed. "I know who you want to ask."

"Shut up."

"You want to ask Amy Murphy." He stared at Simon.

"Shut up."

Tommy nodded. "Okay, but do it early. When she says no, you'll need to find a backup."

When she says no... That was not a confidence booster. But did he even have the confidence to ask her in the first place? She was only the girl he had been crushing on for a year and refusing to talk to because he was too scared.

The ball came rolling up the field, and this time there was no faking it. It was coming right for Simon. Only, he wasn't watching. He was staring off into space as it thudded into his foot and bounced up, smacking him in the face.

All he could think as he watched the ball soar away from his skull was, *I hope Amy doesn't hear about this.*

⚬

Julie's bus stopped on the same corner that they had sledded from. The location raised the question in her mind as she followed Marcy from their seat to the front: Should they do some sledding now? Before the winter sunset came crashing down and they were forced inside?

But when her foot touched the ground and she saw what was happening down the street, she lost the idea of sledding altogether.

Julie stood beside Marcy, Simon, and Tommy. To their right were Harvey and Lee. To their left were a few kids Julie didn't know that well who lived down the hill in the other direction. The bus rumbled and pulled away, and each of them just stared.

Mr. Milton stood on his front porch, talking to a policeman. Another policeman was at Julie's door, talking to her father. Another was knocking on Marcy's door, but Julie was pretty sure there was no one home since Marcy's mom didn't get off work until five.

"What's going on?" Simon asked.

It was a good question. There were police at four different doors on their street, and Mrs. Polson was on her porch again, crying.

"Canvasing the area," Tommy said. "I've seen it on TV. They knock on every door and ask questions about whatever it is."

"What do you think it is?" Simon asked.

"Look." Julie pointed at Mrs. Polson. "They were at her house yesterday."

Tommy nodded. "She killed him."

"What?" they each asked.

"When was the last time you saw Mr. Polson? Sure, she's playing the helpless widow right now, but as soon as the insurance money comes in, she'll be lying in the sun in the Bahamas."

"Shut up." Marcy shook her head. "That's dumb."

"Seen it on TV."

Whatever was happening, Julie was pretty sure Tommy was full of hot air. People didn't get murdered on her street. She lived in a safe place—didn't she? Whatever the police were looking for, it wasn't because of a murder, right?

The cop talking to Mr. Milton stuffed his pad into his pocket and retreated down the porch steps. That was when a few things came to

Julie that she probably would rather have not noticed.

There was something flapping, barely audible, in the gap past her house. Just a thin sliver of yellow plastic fluttered in the wind between her home and the Polsons', and she wished she didn't know what it was: yellow caution tape, the kind police put up when there was a murder.

Then she saw Mr. Milton. His gaze was hard, and though he had to have been like a hundred, his stare didn't show it. He looked up the hill, his focus moving from child to child, examining them, weighing something about each of them, until he stopped at Julie. At her, he stared longer.

There was a hard knowing in that stare, a knowledge that Julie wanted nothing to do with. Just like the sight of that police tape, she would have rather not seen it—or at least, she would have rather been able to forget it.

The old man coughed and grabbed the railing around his porch. For a moment, Julie was worried he was going to collapse, he was shaking so bad as he leaned forward. He coughed so loudly she could hear it from up the street.

"Look." Tommy had spotted the tape. "See, I told you. Murder."

The word hung in Julie's thoughts. *Murder.* She heard it echo, drilling inside her mind the same way that the old man's piercing eyes had.

Murder.

She wanted to climb into bed and cuddle Jynx. She didn't know why, but she was sure he would keep her safe.

December 16th

9 Days 'til Christmas.

Lionel Cobbuge stepped onto his dark front porch and nearly lost his shit. His right foot went sliding hard right, and his left was not ready for that. He grabbed the handrail his grandmother had installed at the behest of his mother—it was a necessity for seventy-plus-year-olds living alone, his mother had insisted—and thankfully, that was enough to keep him from faceplanting into the icy front porch.

"Jesus Christ!" His drunken words echoed through the dark early-morning air, and after he straightened himself upright, he scanned the street to see if anyone had heard him. He might not have been the greatest teacher in the school district, but he was a teacher, and he needed to keep his job. Getting a reputation for being a late-night drunk was not something that would go down well in this community.

The residents of 36th Avenue seemed too tucked in to their cozy little beds to notice his outburst, from what Lionel could see.

"Fuckers." He waved his middle finger at the neighborhood and carefully walked to the front door and fumbled with his keys.

He hated this place. He hated the town. He hated the kids. He hated that he had to rent his dead grandmother's smelly old house from his mother in order to have a place to stay. He hated that he had to take this shitty position as a PE teacher after being forced to resign his previous job as a high school science teacher at Lone Wolf High because he fucked a senior. Granted, he was grateful they didn't have any proof, only rumors, so he didn't get charged, but she wasn't that pretty, anyway. It definitely hadn't been worth it.

He clacked the wrong key into the lock, followed by the right one. There was a crunching sound in the snow behind him, and he spun to see what it was.

Nothing. He wondered for a split second if a nosy neighbor had in fact heard him and was coming to tell him off, but no. There was nothing there.

He grumbled and pushed open the door.

The steps creaked behind him, and the wind rushed inside, carrying an odor that hit his lungs like a brick. It was an odor of death and wetness, of fur and rank musk.

He didn't have time to turn before something hit him in the back that felt like a linebacker from his glory days of high school football. There was a crack in his ribs, and his feet left the living room floor.

Lionel didn't get to make a sound until he slammed into the floor and slid three feet.

"Fuck!" He turned and rolled to see his attacker. Pain shot through his chest and up his neck, then he felt the gashes in his back. They burned.

When his eyes fell on the thing before him, he could neither speak nor move. He was frozen somewhere between terror and disbelief.

It was a cat, but it was the size of a bear. It was black with waves of reddish-brown in its fur and thick, clotted streaks of blood around its mouth. Its massive eyes were locked onto Lionel, and it stood still. Watching. Waiting. Analyzing him.

He saw the black night beyond the cat as a trickle of snow began to fall, carried by a light wind. He wondered if it would cover his tracks inside—this animal's tracks too—when the police came to investigate his death.

He couldn't stop himself from coughing as his lungs suddenly felt full.

Blood slipped from his mouth and spattered over his chest.

That was all it took, the smallest of movements to set the thing into action. A giant paw slid over Lionel's belly, nearly a blur, and his coat, shirt, and skin split apart.

He could see the guts inside him. It was an alien sight, something he should not have been able to see, and as they bulged from the newly opened window, he couldn't stop himself from screaming.

He pushed himself backward. When he tried to move his legs and push, his entire lower half screamed in pain along with him.

Another movement, another blur, this time from the cat's head. It flew downward, seizing his left foot, and in the blink of an eye, the foot was no more. The thing chewed, and a bleeding stump sat at the end of his leg.

"What?" he screamed. He scrambled for words, and none came, only stutters.

Lionel rolled onto his belly and frantically clawed at the living room floor, pulling himself away from the monster.

There was a crunch of meat and bone in his right leg. Then one in his left. He felt something on the right side of his abdomen and then the left.

The attack seemed to have stopped, but he didn't look back. He kept trying to crawl, only traveling inches at a time, but he pulled. He felt his legs gush, and he was on fire all over. He pulled and groaned and, after a few more seconds of nothing clawing at him, he had to turn and see. Had it left?

He was a faint reflection in the giant, black eyes of a monster. It sat there, watching him, almost mocking his pain, and he understood: he was a toy in the mind of the thing. He was no more than a mouse to a house cat, and it was waiting to see what he did next.

What could he do? He had to run but couldn't. He needed a hospital, and there was no way he was going to get to one. His next move was crucial, and he was out of options.

"Fuck you!" he screamed at the thing.

Its lips pulled back, exposing teeth as large as his arm. It dove forward, sinking them into his throat.

He gagged, feeling his windpipe blocked. His neck was hot and wet as it let go.

The good thing was that his pain below the neck went away. Every feeling below there halted, other than a general sensation of cold wetness. The terrifying thing, the thing that made him want to scream but that he had no control to make happen, was that once the cat released his neck and dropped him to the floor, it began eating him from his legs upward.

Lionel's head was left crooked but high enough that he was forced to watch each bite as the monster devoured him.

He was grateful when he had lost enough blood and the blackness came.

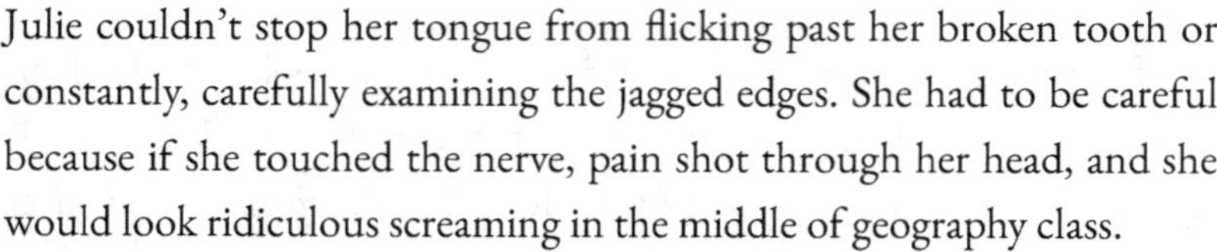

Julie couldn't stop her tongue from flicking past her broken tooth or constantly, carefully examining the jagged edges. She had to be careful because if she touched the nerve, pain shot through her head, and she would look ridiculous screaming in the middle of geography class.

Luckily, they had a video to watch. All of her classes this week seemed more like time-killers than actual classes. Math was just a series of worksheets where, after they did the problems, they colored the coordinating hue into a picture. English was free read, and they were even allowed to read comics, which never happened. And science was just another video. It was like the whole school was just faking it until their break started on

Friday at 2:50.

She was okay with an easy week. She just wished there was something she could do about her tooth.

There was no way Julie was going to tell her mom. Mom had enough to do with Christmas coming, and she was sure there was no money left in the budget for a dentist appointment this month.

She just had to live with the occasional pain when food slipped between the nerve and the opposing tooth, and try to remember to chew on the other side of her mouth. That was what she did last night, and it mostly worked. She was sure Mom thought she didn't like the broccoli when she kept wincing, but she was able to keep herself from screaming, so that was okay.

Besides, she was pretty sure the broken tooth was a baby tooth. That meant it was going to fall out eventually anyway.

She wished that day would hurry up and come.

The screen in the front of the room showed wooded landscapes in Africa somewhere, and Julie drifted into thoughts about lions and tigers. She saw them stalking their prey and attacking the same way Jynx did with her homemade toy, a two-foot length of her mother's yarn and a small stuffed animal she had tied it to.

She smiled, thinking about Jynx. He was so small and cute, and when he cuddled and purred she felt it rumble inside her chest. She wasn't sure where he had disappeared to when she woke up and found he wasn't in bed during the night, but he was there in the morning, so she wasn't worried.

She *was* a little worried about the police cars on her street. There were two there last night, and two were there again this morning.

Simon had asked if Mr. Polson had been murdered at dinner, and Mom and Dad wouldn't answer, not even after both kids were sent upstairs when they came home to cops at the door and Dad answering questions for over twenty minutes.

Then there was Mr. Milton across the street. The way he had stared at her gave her the creeps, even as she sat at her desk thinking about it. With a creepy stare like that, someone might have thought Mr. Milton had something to do with whatever happened to Mr. Polson.

She shivered.

Julie hoped Mr. Polson was okay, even if he did yell at her a lot for being on his lawn—even if it was just to get a lost ball or an airplane.

Maybe he was lost? Julie's grandmother got lost a couple of times in the spring—that was why Mom said she moved to Shady Ridge, the apartments for old people on the west side of town. There was a really pretty view of Mount Custer from her grandmother's window.

She hoped her Grandma was coming to Christmas this year. She usually came on Christmas Eve and sometimes on Christmas morning, but things had been weird since she moved.

The thought of Grandma being there on Christmas somehow shifted. At first, it was warm, like so many memories of past holidays, but then there was an edge on it, something that made her want to back away from the idea.

She wondered if maybe Grandma should stay home this year for Christmas? Maybe that would be safer?

⸻⬥⸻

When Simon lined up with Tommy at the entrance to the gym, where they met at the beginning of every PE period, he expected to see Coach Cabbage waiting with his patented grin—one that only sadists seemed to have. To the class's surprise, they instead had a substitute. They got to stay inside and play in the gym.

"I don't know who to thank, but I'll take it," Tommy said as they sat on the bleachers. The teachers had all left the gym for some reason, so none of the students were too involved in their assigned games.

"Yeah," Simon agreed. He didn't know whether staying inside for gym or the fact that Amy Murphy said she would go to the movies with him was the best news of the day, but he was thrilled for them both.

His sneakers squeaked as he rotated and took the seat beside Tommy.

"Maybe it's a serial killer?" Tommy said. His eyes bulged, and his smile brightened. "First they got Mr. Polson, and now Coach Cabbage."

Simon shook his head. "He's not dead. Just sick or somethin'."

"Just wait. Last night, the cops were asking about *seeing anything strange in the neighborhood.* I bet tomorrow we get asked again."

Simon's forehead wrinkled. "Is that what they asked? My parents wouldn't say."

Tommy rolled his eyes. "I listened from the dining room. Mr. Polson's missing, and they have no clue why. It's usually the spouse, but now that there's two bodies..."

"We don't even know that Cabbage is missing."

"Just wait."

A whistle blew from the far side of the gym. Standing at the entrance doors were the substitute, the principal, Mrs. Winston, and a pair of police officers. They all looked nervous.

"Told ya." Tommy used his usual *I-told-you-so* voice. It was high, almost a whine, and Simon hated the sound of it.

When Mrs. Winston started her walk into the center of the gym and the class parted to make way for her, the other adults followed. The look of sincere concern on her face struck Simon in a way he was not expecting. The announcement that Coach Cabbage was missing hit even harder, and Simon found himself actually feeling concerned too.

Was Tommy really right? Was there a serial killer on the loose in Custer

Falls?

———◆O◆———

That night, there wasn't quite a curfew, but the word had spread through town to look out for anything strange. Julie, who had never once locked the front door, made sure she had done so when she went up to bed.

She lay in the dim light of her night light, her fingers running through Jynx's soft hair, and having him there made her feel a little better.

He kneaded his little feet on her comforter, and he smashed his head into her chin as he purred. She squeezed him just a little, enough for him to know she loved him but not enough to hurt her baby boy.

Unlike how her parents worried in their rooms about what was going on in their town, she drifted easily to sleep. She didn't notice when Jynx slipped out later on; neither did her family. The only one who did was the across-the-street neighbor with the creepy stare, Mr Milton.

DECEMBER 17TH

IT WAS LONG AFTER midnight before Adam Milton saw what he was looking for. He peeked through the blinds that dressed his front window, the lights off in his living room to hide his surveillance. There was movement in the snow below the Butler house's front hedges, then a dime-sized shine that could only have been the beast's eyes.

His free hand went to his chest, bracing himself, warning his lungs that now was the time for caution. The beast had been gracious the other night, possibly visiting for the simple reason of curiosity, investigating a smell it had not encountered in decades. He did not want to push his luck with the beast's nature—or its hunger. Captive lions had been known to attack those they were familiar with, even loved.

The tiny creature shot into the night, across the lawn, and into the next yard. It was a flash over the snow, and if Adam hadn't been watching with unblinking concentration, he was sure he would have missed it.

It ran through the Burrows' yard, headed up the street, and Adam felt an itch in his throat, accompanied by a rattle in his lungs. He had to know where the beast was going, but he also had to maintain his secrecy—his safety. He tried to suppress what he knew was coming, holding his breath while tracking the beast as it crossed the next yard.

Then, maybe the worst thing that could have happened, happened.

The first in a series of guttural, hacking coughs erupted from Adam's mouth. They were wet and heavy, compressing his lungs and jerking his

"

entire body into uncontrollable spasms.

He yanked his hand away from the window, but he saw his fears come to fruition before the lifted slat dropped back into place.

The cat stopped mid-stride, frozen in the center of a giant patch of snow, its head pivoting, its eyes zeroing in on the out-of-place sound in that black night. Its gaze stilled on Adam's house, on his window. And the slat sealed Adam's view of the outside world.

He doubled over, leaning on his knees for support as the unstoppable wave of expulsion seized him. His throat burned and his chest pained. He tasted blood through the phlegm, and he cursed his sickness and his choices—he thought about his last days and wished he had made better decisions in his life. He prayed, though, that he had dropped the slat in time. He saw the blood on the floor in that distant memory, and he prayed that that wasn't his destiny. As much as he hated his sickness, he feared the pain of what he had seen worse.

The cough subsided, and he managed to keep himself conscious. He held himself still in that same position, hands on knees, leaning forward, his fingers digging into his legs to maintain his balance.

He listened.

He needed to know if it was coming, and he had to be silent. He had made one noise, shown himself, and it could have been listening for another. He wanted to look out that window and see the thing tearing up the street—as selfish as it was, he wanted to know that it was hunting someone other than him.

There was no sound. Even his wet, rattling breaths were paused, no matter the strain and burn in his chest.

His ears rang with soft age-induced tinnitus. The wind rustled between the leaves of the hedge outside his window, and until it stopped, his heart fluttered with the uncertainty of not knowing if that sound was the cat in disguise. A quick whip of wind made the ceiling creak.

Adam took a deep breath. His eyes circled the room's vast shadows, looking for any sign of an intruder. He sniffed, daring his nose to find the musty scents that had filled his house days prior—and years before that.

Nothing.

Could he have been that lucky? His mother always said it was better to be lucky than smart. Daring the monster by watching it through that lifted slat was not smart. Wasn't surviving it twice enough without pushing his luck any further?

He let himself collapse into his chair, unable to stop the memory from crashing over him.

——◆◇◆——

8 Days 'til Christmas, 1968.

Amma Freydís stoked the fire in the living room. It was a cold night, colder than it was supposed to have been, and eight-year-old Adam knew something was wrong with his grandmother, no matter what excuses his mother gave.

"Jesus, how hot do you want it?" Father snapped from his chair. He ruffled his paper and went back to reading.

Father was in no mood tonight, and Adam had already had his rump turned red for talking back during dinner. He hadn't thought he was talking back just for asking how his father knew the Apollo rockets were all a scheme to intimidate the commies, but Father took it that way.

Adam should have known from the whiskey-scented breath crossing the table to keep his mouth shut and his head down that night. His little brother, Paul, even flinched during the remark. Maybe he screwed up because he was on edge from the killings over the last few days—they all were.

Everyone had a theory. Jonny Dawson said it was Martians. His teacher, Mrs. Willits, said it was likely a drifter—a view propagated by the Lone Wolf Police Department. Amma said they were all wrong, and Mother hushed her every time she opened her mouth.

Mother didn't like it when Amma talked about folklore from the old country. For one, it irritated Father, but more than that, Mother had grown up hearing those old stories, and whenever she brought them up in her own life, her American friends looked at her funny, even laughed at her. They were make-believe and old-fashioned nonsense. They were remnants of an older, less-enlightened time, and after the embarrassment Mother felt for once believing her own mother, she wasn't going to allow Amma to infect her children with it.

It wasn't until after the blood spilled that Amma explained.

Sometime after Adam and Paul went to sleep, a clatter startled them both awake. It was like a crash, and Adam's immediate thought was that someone had driven a car into the side of the house.

He jumped out of his bed and ran to the door. He peeked into the hallway and jumped when he felt his brother's breath on the back of his arm.

"What happened?" Paul was rubbing sleep from his eyes.

"I don't know." Adam stepped into the hallway.

He had a narrow view into the living room, but he could see light flickering and the edge of Father's chair. There was a smell in the air that was thick and pungent, something that made the hair on the back of his neck rise. That smell made him want to run back to his bed, but he couldn't. He needed to know what was happening. He started down the hall and stopped in his tracks when he heard a scream.

It was a noise like he had never heard in his life. It was a human sound, but there was so much emotion behind it he could have thought an animal had made it, a pained, rabid animal lost somewhere in primal agony.

A dark-red hand reached around the corner, and Adam heard the noise again. Then Father's bloody face rounded the corner.

The man fell forward, leaving bloody handprints on the light-blue rug that trimmed the hall. He saw his sons and reached for them, then his mouth opened to its widest, and that same horrifying sound bellowed, reverberating in the narrow space and paining Adam's ears.

Blood shot from between Father's lips, and his voice turned into a garbled, watery noise. His eyes pleaded with Adam to save him. His lips trembled as his head dropped to the floor.

Father's body was torn out of sight, vanishing around the corner.

Adam screamed as something touched his shoulder. He spun and saw his brother hiding his eyes as his mouth moved a mile a minute, saying nothing. His amma's hand was on him. She held a finger over her lips, warning him to be as quiet as she was.

A splat hit the carpet, and Adam spun again. It was a pile of blood and hunks of something he could not recognize.

He was about to speak, then, remembering his grandmother's warning, sealed his mouth with his hand.

He heard sounds of wet crunching. Chewing. Ripping. He wanted to dart back into his room, but something told him he was better off staying still, being silent.

The floor creaked the way it did when Father walked across the living room. He was a large, heavy man, and Adam had thought that only his father could force the floor to make that sound. The thought brought him hope for a second—maybe he had mistaken what he had seen? Maybe it was a trick?

The beast strode between the edges of the slim view Adam had into his living room, and the second it took for the thing to pass felt like a lifetime. The fear that seized his guts, praying it would not turn and see him, the smell that he now recognized belonged to a monster, the sound of its giant feet quietly gliding over the wooden floor, all permanently carved themselves into his memory.

The black and reddish-brown coat screamed death. The swagger of its body was that of a prideful hunter. The whip of its tail was fanciful yet packed with power. The whiskers, like thick cords, extended beyond its body like dozens of spears.

It left, and they didn't move. Not for as long as it took for the ocean of blood that coated his living room floor to flood into the hall. It was like a monster of its own, the way it slowly enveloped the blue carpet that Adam's mother took such pride in cleaning every Monday and Thursday, inching its way toward them as if they were on its menu.

When they were sure the monster was gone, really gone, Adam and his amma ventured into the living room. She didn't want him to go, but he would not take no for an answer, and he was the man of the house now. He had already seen what death had brought. If he insisted, she would say he was due.

There was nothing left of Father unless he counted the various strings and pee-sized chunks of flesh, and those he couldn't tell whom they belonged to.

A single hand remained of Mother. Her left. It still held her wedding ring.

In his chair, almost six decades later, holding his aged chest, Adam realized that he didn't cry after seeing those things. Something inside him hardened that day, and the gore he had witnessed became abstract objects more than pieces of his parents. But even so, he recognized that that fear and those sights had returned a thousand times over the next sixty years, even if only through shadows of feelings and blurs in his thoughts and dreams.

He could no longer hide behind the wall he put up when he was eight. At sixty-five, he would have to truly face them. There was no longer any doubt of that.

<hr>

When Julie got home from school on the 17th, she didn't think she had ever been so happy to be back. She went straight to her room, straight to her bed, where she could sit and cuddle her Jynxie.

As soon as her rump touched the bed, he was in her lap, stretching, purring, and kneading.

School had been controlled more than she ever remembered. The halls between classes flowed quickly with teachers at every corner, watching and guiding. Exits were monitored all day, even the cafeteria and east-side exits, which only led to the school's contained inner courtyard. There was no outside time, no after-school activities, and they were all herded directly into buses as soon as the last bell rang.

Simon said his day was similar. Everyone was on edge, teachers on guard, and each kid wore a shell of apprehension.

On the bus, Tommy declared he was right again, that there was, in fact, a serial killer and that another person had gone missing the previous night.

No one wanted to believe Tommy, but his news left them all sitting in silence for several minutes.

Julie was just happy to be back at home. She knew that whatever was going on out in that cold, dark world was beyond those walls. She knew that as long as she was inside and had her boy in her lap that she was safe.

There was a tingling feeling inside telling her that that wasn't quite true, but she wasn't going to listen to it. She was home. She was warm.

She had her boy, and that was all that mattered at that moment.

She couldn't help but notice that her boy was a little bit bigger today. She knew kittens grew fast, but she would have guessed that if she weighed him, he had put on a pound or more.

And he smelled a bit different. A bit musty, like something wild—just a bit.

DECEMBER 18TH

7 Days 'til Christmas.

CHRISTMAS WAS A WEEK away, and despite the strange disappearances in town—and for some reason, them being focused around a few-block radius in eastern Custer Falls—Julie and nearly every kid in her class was more excited than ever for the big day to come.

It wasn't just for presents—or, sure, for some kids it was—to Julie, it was about the entire Christmas vacation that was just hours away. It was about sledding without worrying about having school the next day. It was about sharing hot chocolate with Marcy and knowing there was nothing else for them to do but have fun. It was about a long break with freedom from routines.

Most importantly, though, it was about Mom and Dad, about the smiles on Christmas Eve, about the love in the air on Christmas morning as they shivered just so slightly after rising from bed and waiting for Dad to build the living room fire. Then Julie and Simon would help Mom get the cinnamon rolls on the pan and into the oven as Dad made the grownups coffee. It was a ritual, and each moment of it was one they shared in anticipation and love.

Of course, then, with classic Christmas music in the background, they would rip into everything. There would be a few new toys, and there would be some necessities, some clothes that they desperately needed which, after opening, would get set aside and not touched again until they had to put them away. There would be some gifts that had been used before Mom found them, and Julie and Simon would know just how ridiculously much she was devoted to them, that she had to have spent hours combing through the thrift stores looking for things she knew her kids would enjoy, even if they could never afford them new.

Then they would sit there. Mom and Dad would cuddle on the couch. Julie and Simon would examine and play with each present a little more, getting to know every item inside and out. They would enjoy the warmth of the fire and the warmth of each other in a way that was distinctly Christmas morning and special, a time that was different than all the other moments they shared.

Plus, this year she had Jynxie. She imagined him crawling through the torn paper and playing with abandoned bows. He would stalk and attack the discarded stuffing and crumpled balls of wrappings, and hopefully not bring down the tree if he got too wild.

As she sat in science class, and the video about photosynthesis droned on, she watched the animated plants rise on screen. Julie considered how much Jynx was growing. Last night he was definitely bigger, and when she picked him up this morning, he felt bigger still. She would swear he was a three- or four-month-old cat from the added length and girth, not one that was only eight or nine weeks old as she had been told. But he was a free cat Mom had found somewhere in town, meowing in a box that read *Free Kittens!* They didn't even know what breed he was. Maybe he was one of those giant cats she had heard about, and his growth spurt was perfectly normal?

The bell rang with the movie still playing, and Mr. Freed simply waved the class away from his desk. "See you tomorrow. One more day!" That brought cheers from students as they gathered their things.

One more day. The words resonated in Julie's mind, and her heart rate rose. *One more day.* She couldn't wait.

Erica Butler took a bite of the sandwich she had made that morning for her lunch and changed lanes. If she was going to make this trip work, she would have to keep a tight eye on traffic and her interactions. She had fifty-four minutes left in her lunch hour to make it to the other side of town (while eating), go inside Shady Ridge (hoping their staff would acknowledge her at a decent pace), visit with her mother (and decide if she thought Mom was up to the visit on Christmas Eve), and then get back to work (without Stanley noticing she had completely left the property). She was going to be cutting it close; she knew that.

Forty-six minutes left: Sandwich done and half her chips eaten, she pulled up to the retirement home.

Forty-one minutes left: After waiting for the front desk attendant's attention and them verifying where her mother was (even though Erica already knew her mother's routine and told them), she was escorted to the reading nook in the memory-care wing, where her mother spent every afternoon between lunch and activity time.

Thirty-five minutes left: She approached Mom.

Mom flipped the page of the large print edition of *Gone with the Wind*, the book that had rotated through Erica's house as a child and adolescent, moving from bookshelf to coffee table to Mom's nightstand over and over again. It was her mother's favorite, one she could recite the words from, chapter and verse, better than some of the most devout could recite the beginning of the book of Genesis. The book was as much a member of the family as Erica's brother, Charles, God rest his soul.

But Mom wasn't quite reading it.

She sat in her seat, as she did every day, and started with chapter one. Her eyes ran past the words on the page as sixteen-year-old Scarlett O'Hara sat on her Southern plantation's porch, and not soon after turning the page, Erica's mother stopped, turned back to the beginning of chapter one, and started all over again.

It broke Erica's heart every time she saw it, and she forced the tears back as she sat down beside her mother.

"Mom?" She placed a hand on her mother's knee. "How are you doing today?"

Mom looked up and smiled. It was the smile of fake recognition, the type of smile you might give to a waitress or someone claiming to be an old high school classmate that you have absolutely no recollection of. Then she blinked and tilted her head left just a bit, and the smile faded, exchanged for a brief look of disgust before it dropped away in favor of fake congeniality.

Those were the looks Erica was waiting for. They were the looks her mother had given her since she married Scott against her advice and settled into what would become a life of meager subsistence filled with love, instead of Mom's suggestion of going to college in Missoula, fighting to afford it, with the goal of marrying a man enrolled in pre-med. Erica's mother wanted children with money, and to that effect, both Erica and Charles had failed her.

"Hello, dear." She placed her hand over Erica's and patted it softly. "How are you doing?"

The familiar words and gentle touch were a veneer over contempt, a tactic Erica had grown a thick skin to endure. She didn't let it get to her—not there, anyway. At home, alone in the tub, that might be another story, after she had time to herself. But this woman was her mother, and despite the way Mom felt about her, she loved the woman. She would respect her. And she wasn't there for herself. She was there for the kids.

Erica didn't have grandparents growing up. She saw other kids who did, kids with extra sets of loving relatives that she didn't have, and she wanted that for her children. So much so that she overlooked the behaviors her mother brought to the table, behaviors she taught herself not to emulate.

Like the beatings for not keeping her room pristine. Like the passive-aggressive digs for not doing as well as a parent would have liked. Like the backhanded compliments that made every one of her achievements feel somehow minuscule compared to the bar her mother set.

Erica leaned back in her seat. "Oh, you know, getting ready for Christmas."

Her mother blinked, likely calculating the time of year. She was always a proud woman, too proud to admit defeat at anything and too proud to ask for help.

"It sure is coming up fast," Mom said. "I bet the children will sure enjoy it. You do such a great job fitting in affordable gifts with your job."

Twenty-eight minutes left: Erica bit her tongue.

"Do you feel like coming for Christmas Eve this year? The nurse says that as long as you're feeling up to it, she approves."

"Well, I'm glad we have *her* permission." Mom grinned.

"Mom..."

"I think it would be lovely to spend the evening in your beautiful home. You always do decorate so tastefully for the holidays." That was bullshit. She was trying to play nice, maybe to get out of the home, but they both knew Mom thought every Christmas decoration Erica owned was tacky garbage.

But Erica let it all roll off her back. It was for the kids—the decorations, the activities, even bringing Mom home was for the kids.

"Wonderful."

Twenty-six minutes left, twice what she needed: Erica stood. "I'll let the nurse know, and I'll see you next week."

"Wonderful." Mom didn't wait for Erica to leave. She raised her book and started back on chapter one.

Erica didn't cry—not on the way out, not on the way back to work. She would hold it in until the kids were in bed and she had the tub to herself.

———◄○►———

Scott Butler sat at the computer in his room and logged into the online data entry portal he had signed up for a month ago to earn some extra spending money for the holidays. He didn't think he would be able to do more than an hour of work today, but he was going to try.

He was lucky; it looked like the Internet was behaving today. They could only afford the lowest tier of broadband speed, and some days, that was so slow he barely qualified for the work.

The application came up as did the scanned-in data for him to transfer. The job was boring and tedious, but it was simple and easy, and with him never knowing how his nerves would fare, he was starting to like having the opportunity.

He had entered his third invoice into the system when he heard the bedroom door squeak. That was odd because he was sure that he had shut it. Glancing over, he saw a small brown paw slip between the door and the jamb and push it open enough for the cat to slip his head into the room.

The feline looked at Scott, locking his stare on the man at the computer. There was something going on in that stare, something the cat was calculating, and Scott wasn't sure if he liked it.

He had been okay with the idea of getting the cat, more so than Erica.

They were both concerned about the costs: vet bills, food, toys, all that. But when they compared those costs to how long Julie had been asking for a cat and how happy they knew it would make her... He would be keeping this boring Internet job as long as he had to to afford the thing.

But the way it was looking at him was odd. He was no stranger to cats and expected this one to either jump up on his lap for petting or decide it wanted nothing to do with him, but not what it did next.

"How are you today, Jynx?" he asked the cat in a singsong voice. He smiled, knowing he was being dumb but hoping to bridge the gap. They were likely going to be roommates for a long time, after all.

The cat just watched him, unmoving from the cracked door.

"Okay. I have to get this work done while the pain's at a low roar, so..." He turned back to the computer and rolled his eyes. "I'm talking to a cat..."

He put the cat out of his mind and went back to work. After entering another invoice, he felt a soft press on his thigh.

The cat was standing on his hind legs, front paws on Scott's leg. He was waiting.

Scott lifted his arm, making room for the cat to jump, and it did, right up onto his lap. Scott nodded and, not trying to pressure the animal, went back to work.

Two more things struck Scott as odd while he typed. The cat in his lap felt twice as heavy as it should have been. He remembered seeing the thing when Erica brought it into the house, and there was no way that scrawny kitten weighed this much—he wondered how much Julie had been feeding him.

The second thing was the smell. The cat didn't smell like any house cat he had ever known, not even when the litter box was ripe and in need of a change. He wondered if it had gotten out of the house and been sprayed by a skunk or something.

Either way, Julie was going to have to teach him what a bath was.

As if Jynx was reading his mind, claws instantly went into Scott's legs, and the cat sprang from his lap and darted out of the room.

The sting was instantaneous, and red spots dotted Scott's pants.

All he could do was grit his teeth and keep working. Working through the pain was what Scott did.

***

Sunset came and then the snow, but the showers faded away. The moon stood watch over the star-lit sky, and the new crystals shimmered across the city. With the spreading worry of a killer on the loose, the streets were bare long before midnight. It let Jynx come out, leaving small pawprints in the fresh white blanket earlier than the past few nights.

He sniffed the air and scanned the street, then he was up the hill. He sprinted from yard to yard, pausing in the brush every so often, recalculating his path and verifying just who was and wasn't around.

He paused longer after he crossed Railroad. Was his quarry where he thought it was? Was it on the move? Or was it just the wind?

He didn't make a sound louder than his paws pressing into the snow as he sprang down Railroad Street and—

December 19th

—ducked behind a pair of large green trash cans.

— ◆ —

Midnight had ticked by, and Carol LeMonte was still cursing and tossing aside clothes from the couch, trash from the kitchen counter, and... It occurred to her she had not searched Josh's room. She was late to work by over an hour, late to a job that put food on the table for her and Josh—the only thing keeping the wolves at bay—and there she was still trying to find her damn car keys.

She stormed down the hall toward the sound of her son's speed metal playlist, which was barely muffled by the thin walls in the small two-bedroom house. Music often meant Josh was still awake, but who knew? It wasn't uncommon for him to drift off for the night with his stereo blaring.

It wasn't that she liked her job. In fact, she hated it. It was boring and monotonous, and anyone she told about it usually politely refrained from stating their outright distaste for her situation. She stocked the shelves overnight at the big-box department-slash-grocery store that everyone hated, and as soon as she mentioned that it was where she worked, people just assumed it meant she was a less-than, that she must be unintelligent, that she was a bad mother, and that she was a low-class person and should either be pitied or avoided.

That was fine. She didn't need those people in her life. She did what she had to do to take care of herself and her kid, and if people had a problem with that, fuck 'em. She didn't need anyone's approval for how she lived her life or how she raised her kid, even if he was a little shit.

She was sure that he stole that gun from the pastor. She was sure that they were right to kick him out of school and make him wait for approval to transfer to the only other high school in town while the situation was resolved. He *was* a little shit. But he was *her* little shit, so, of course, she lied to the police. Of course, she screamed at that pastor and told him he was full of shit. Yes, she told the school board she was going to sue them, regardless of the fact that she had no lawyer and no way to afford one.

If anyone was going to beat her son down, it was going to be her, and not them. She was the one cursed with his existence since birth; she was the one who had to starve him to get him to eat the stuff she wanted him to eat when he was little; she was the one who had to beat him almost nightly with a belt to keep him in line until he was too big and could fight back. It was her job to make him behave, not theirs.

Carol flung open Josh's door, hoping to god he wasn't masturbating or something as she did it—and also kind of hoping he was, to scare the kid and teach him a lesson about losing her things.

"Where are my goddamn keys?" she screamed over the music.

Josh looked up from the bed with a contentious glare, raising his eyes over his comic but not giving her the respect of actually acting as if she mattered more than an annoying little sister breaking into his space.

"I don't have your *goddamn keys*," he mocked.

She rolled her eyes, looked on his cluttered dresser and messy bed. The floor was coated in dirty clothes, crumbs, and other trash. She stepped inside, moved a few things around on the dresser, only spotting more trash and a scattered carton's worth of condoms.

"Clean your goddamn room," she barked.

If the keys were in there, it would take a miracle to find them, and she needed them right now. She decided to give her room one more search.

Carol stepped inside her room, closed her eyes, and took a deep breath. She opened them, walked over to her dresser, and scanned the spaces between empty wine glasses, makeup, and candles. About a third of the way down the surface, she spotted a bright-red bottle opener attached with a ring to a full-to-overflowing keyring.

She stared down at the splayed array of every key she had owned in her thirty-five years of life, including her car keys.

"Shit."

She shook her head and snagged the keys. The jingle was so loud she expected to hear Josh howl at her from his bedroom as soon as she turned to go. Apparently, his music was loud enough that she was saved the embarrassment.

Out through her door and into the hallway, past his door, and almost to the living room, she was at full speed toward the front door and on the way to work. That was when it happened.

Something so hot it seemed to sizzle grabbed her from behind. It hooked into her shoulder and yanked her from her feet.

Carol smelled something dense and strong. It was almost so shocking that she forgot about her shoulder—almost.

Falling, she reached up and left, trying to grab whatever was holding her, and when she was almost to the floor, she saw something that did distract her from her shoulder.

Staring down into Carol's eyes was a thing of horrifying magnificence. It was so captivating, she thudded on the hallway carpet before she screamed.

The thick fur, the haunting eyes the size of dishes, those were bad enough, but the teeth she saw as it opened its mouth were as large as her forearm. The dark, damp tongue inside its mouth was lined with hooks. The breath that came from its spreading maw smelled like something between rotting fish and an old, bloody pile of hamburger.

And it stared into her eyes like it was waiting for her reaction before it took its next step.

The hallway light beyond the thing shifted, and she lowered her gaze. Josh was in his doorway, staring into the hall. His eyes were frozen, bulging, and his mouth hung open. He was staring at this monstrous thing in their house with as much shock and terror as Carol.

Suddenly, the fear inside her skyrocketed. It was enough to have a monster hovering over her; it was something else to know her vulnerable son was five feet away. He was a shit—that was true—but he was *her* shit.

Carol reached up as fast as she could, forming a fist and punching the monster in the jaw with a swing barely hard enough to knock one of those wine glasses from her dresser, but with the pain in her shoulder and punching from the floor, it was all she could muster.

It was enough to keep its attention. It was enough to buy her time to scream, "Shut your door and run!"

She didn't see if he shut his door. She saw the monster take her hand in its mouth, and she yanked back a stump, bloody and pulsing blood.

Carol screamed, and the beast planted its head into her chest. A wave of overwhelming agony left her shaking and helpless. She couldn't suck in air. Her house faded around her, leaving a dim tunnel of sight as she watched the thing's jaws open and close over her midsection.

Her mouth twitched. She imagined she looked like a fish trying to breathe air. She imagined her son jumping from his window and running. She hoped that was happening.

At 4:05 p.m., when Julie stepped from her bus with a backpack full of books she wouldn't need for more than two weeks, she could smell the freedom in the air. Granted, that freedom smelled like smoke from the nearby houses with wood stoves, but to her it meant home, vacation, and liberty the way the Founding Fathers must have intended.

"Yes!" Simon shouted as his feet touched the icy pavement.

"School's out!" Tommy said, planting his boots beside Simon's. He glanced at his phone. "And two and a half hours until movie time."

"Movie time?" Marcy asked. "You still think your parents will let you go with all the missing people?"

"Yours won't?" He gave her a snide stare. "Just tell your mom there will be like twenty kids there, and you get safety in numbers. Tell her everyone's going, and you'll be the weirdo outcast if you don't show up."

"Won't be enough," Simon said. "I know my mom, and she would normally let us walk, but..."

"Okay," Tommy raised his hands. "Just tell her my mom is driving us. Drop off right at the theater door. Pick up at the same door two hours later."

"I don't know."

"You have to go! Don't make me do this date thing alone."

Simon sighed. "I'll try."

"How do you think Amy's going to react if you stand her up? This is your shot..."

After he got home, Simon did more than try. He made the case to his mom and dad, and they said no. Then Julie made the same case, and they thought about it more. When both Simon and Julie begged together, Erica Butler finally gave in under the exact stipulation Tommy had suggested: door-to-door service from Tommy's mom.

⎯⎯◆◇◆⎯⎯

The drop off had Julie excited. If everyone who said they would showed up to the movies, it would be like a takeover of the theater. She wasn't necessarily interested in the movie itself, some animated thing for kids five years younger than her; it was the experience she was hyped for.

The sun had set, and night had secured its embrace over Custer Falls. It was early, but with the dark cloud cover and the sun long gone, it was hard to imagine that the day had just faded.

Julie stood beside the ticket line, and a snowflake hit her nose. It tickled and distracted her from the growing crowd. When another touched her cheek, and the cold ran along her skin, she gazed up into the sky, and hope filled her heart. Maybe the worst of things was behind them? Maybe the disappearances would stop, and they would be free to enjoy their Christmas?

She would stay positive. That was what Mom would do.

She looked across the ticket line. So many faces were smiling. Simon stood with Amy, and Tommy with Robin. Ben was with Marcy, and another dozen kids from sixth and seventh grade filled the line. The air had a crispness to it, and a feeling of gratitude and expectation hung over them all now that school was out for the next two weeks and only fun lay ahead.

How could she not feel hopeful?

Josh LeMonte pulled his coat tighter around his chest as the snow started falling. That was the worst thing he could have asked for; he was already freezing.

After running from his house in the middle of the night and spending the day bouncing from place to place just trying to stay warm and avoiding the police—he was sure they already found what was left of his mother and assumed that he did it—he just wanted a warm spot to sit and rest for a little while.

He slipped through the alley between the downtown walking mall and the carousel and spotted the back entrance to Custer Falls's movie theater. He supposed if he could slip inside a movie he might be able to catch a little bit of rest and get warm. It was worth a shot, anyway.

Julie took her ticket from Marcy, and together, they walked into the lobby. Marcy barely looked at Julie, she was so focused on Ben, but that was okay. Julie was really just there as a wingman type of thing, a little bit of security and backup if Marcy needed it.

Marcy and Ben got in the popcorn line, and Julie took a seat on a bench by the plate-glass windows that separated the lobby from the outside world. She had told Marcy that she wasn't hungry, but the fact was she couldn't afford any snacks. And truthfully, she was still scared to eat more than she had to with her broken tooth always threatening to stab her with pain. Still, she didn't let that bother her. She was happy to watch the snow land on the people in the ticket line and collect on the tree in the center of the drop-off roundabout.

She heard Marcy laugh as she saw her brother, Amy, Tommy, and Robin walk through the front door with their tickets in hand.

Then there was a scream.

Every person in the lobby turned left toward the first hallway of theaters. A man, a woman, and a teenager were running into the lobby, each with fear dripping from their faces.

Julie watched them all as, one by one, they looked back the way they had come. She noticed the man and woman both had dark-red dots all over their clothes and their faces, and the teenager was actually Josh LeMonte, the boy about whom so many rumors had been floating around. And something was chasing them.

The patrons in the lobby stared, none of them understanding what was going on and all of them glued to the scene. They were like a room full of mannequins, not people, and the closer the group fleeing the hallway came, the more the tension rose.

Julie's eyes met Josh's, and he observed the crowded room. He opened his mouth and said one word. "Run!"

No one moved. Either they were too stunned, too incredulous at the idea that something important was actually happening, or too entranced by the moment to understand what he was saying.

Julie, however, put more together than she wanted. The blood on their faces, the running, the screaming... Whatever was happening was dangerous.

She grabbed Marcy by the hand and pulled, and Marcy tried to resist but was no match for Julie's intensity. They took a step toward the hallway on the right, and something leaped on top of the blood-spattered man.

It was something from a nightmare. It was huge and wild, moving like a cat but the size of a bear. It squished the man to the floor and leaped from him, its rear claws slicing him nearly in half as it flew at the woman.

The lobby exploded in screams. Workers ducked behind the counter. The patrons in the hall split into two groups, half headed for the front door, half toward the same hall of theaters Julie was trying for. A couple entering through the front door froze in place and were shoved aside by kids trying to escape. The man slipped in the snow, dragging his date to the ground, and exiting kids stomped on them as they ran.

Loud pops broke through the screams, and Julie stopped a few feet into the hall. She ducked into the alcove that held the bathrooms. Marcy scurried past, not stopping until she was inside the women's restroom.

What Julie saw verified the rumors about the teen boy, but not how she expected. Josh stood in front of the snack bar holding a gun and pointing it at the gigantic cat, and he was firing at it.

The beast stared at Josh as if trying to understand him. It stood on the woman it just tackled, one giant paw on her chest, blood bubbling up between its foot and her body as she jerked and trembled. It did this while Josh's bullets flew into it.

The scene was unreal. The noise repeated as Josh pulled the trigger. Tufts of fur puffed up and flared out, and small spatterings of blood bloomed from the impacts—but the monster was unfazed. It didn't move. It was obviously being struck, but once the shot was over and its fur settled down, it was like nothing whatsoever had happened.

Josh's gun locked back. He was out of bullets.

About five people, three kids and two adults, fought to get out through the front door. Six moviegoers sat on the floor, backs against walls and windows where they had been pushed or fallen when the cat stormed in. A man held his chest and gasped on the cold tile floor by the snack counter.

"Die, you motherfucker!" Josh squeezed the trigger, and nothing erupted from his barrel. He was out of ammo, but the fact was yet to sink in. Tears ran down his face, and his lips trembled. "You killed her!"

The beast crawled off the woman and took a step in his direction.

"Fuck you!" Josh spun the gun around and threw it at the monster.

The weapon thumped on the giant cat's shoulder and clattered on the ground. The beast looked down at the thing, and Josh charged the gap between them with a knife in his hand. He jumped and buried the blade in the monster's shoulder.

The giant cat snarled and planted its mouth over Josh's shoulder and chest. It lifted the teenager into the air and shook him back and forth like a dog would shake a chew toy.

When the blood started running down Josh's chest and splashing across the room, Julie pulled herself back and slipped into the bathroom.

She whimpered and looked for Marcy. Her friend had locked herself in a stall and was weeping.

Julie didn't know what happened to her brother. Did he make it outside? Was he hiding in a theater? She didn't see the monster get him, but she just didn't know for sure.

What about Tommy? Amy? Robin? Ben? She couldn't remember if she saw anything happen to them or if they escaped.

And she couldn't go back out there and find out. Her body wouldn't let her if she tried to. Her joints burned, and her stomach was rocky. She had done nothing but hide, yet she felt like she had fought in a boxing match.

Julie sat on the floor outside Marcy's stall, her eyes on the restroom door, waiting for whatever was coming next.

DECEMBER 20TH

5 Days 'til Christmas.

IT WAS AFTER MIDNIGHT before Julie got home. She would have fallen asleep in the car if she hadn't been shaking and expecting that monster to emerge from every shadow she passed.

Mom drove to the theater to pick her and Simon up, and the look on her face—the worry—was heartbreaking. Julie didn't think she had ever been squeezed so hard as when Mom hugged her in that parking lot while they were bathed in first responder strobe lights.

About the same time, Marcy's mom came for her, and every other kid's parents as well. The police insisted that their proper guardians pick them up—except for Ben and his older sister, Robin. They were somehow missing. A man who had been huddled on the floor said the monster ate some of the kids—he didn't know which ones—and some of the dead adults too. One of the others in the lobby said something similar. Two others just shook and cried and refused to talk to anyone.

The cops didn't believe Julie or Marcy. They didn't believe any of the witnesses who told the truth. One of the higher-ups, a detective, Julie assumed, said it was something like a mass hallucination or something, like the trauma of Josh opening fire in the theater gave everyone a mental meltdown.

Julie almost believed him at one point. But what she saw... That was too real to have been imagined.

Mom parked, and Julie just sat in the car, staring into the night. She could see the monster out there, hiding in the darkness, waiting for her to step outside so it could grab her and sink its claws into her.

Something touched her, and she screamed.

It was Simon, a soft hand on her. "Come on inside."

Mom was watching them from the front seat. "Come on. You can snuggle with me tonight if you want to."

Julie didn't want to move. There was just too much dark between the car and the house.

Then she saw him.

The light was on in her room, and a soft-pink hue was cast over the window. There was a shadow on the sill, a little silhouette that melted her heart.

Her little boy was up there waiting for her.

He was in her bed when Julie walked into her room. He stood, stretching his front legs and standing tall, eyes wide and head tilted. He meowed as she came closer, reaching with a single, open paw.

"Oh, I'm coming." She leaned down and rubbed his head and scratched his back. He purred and arched toward her. "Just a second."

She quickly changed into her pajamas and crawled into bed. The covers were comforting, her soft sheets and blanket warming her up. And then, there he came. He pressed himself into her chest as he lay beside her, engine running and rubbing the top of his head into her chin.

"Yes, yes." She stroked him and felt the day's horror fade ever so slightly.

She saw the blood on the floor. She saw Josh blasting away and that monster coming toward him like his bullets were just foam projectiles from Simon's toy guns. She saw the woman it had jumped on—screaming—and, as if for the first time, as she thought about that scene, she remembered things she hadn't noticed at the time: the stripes in the cat's fur, like a giant, darker tabby; the gleam in its eyes as it sized up Josh and everyone else in the room; the white spot at the very tip of its massive, swaying tail.

That thought brought her back to her boy. She looked him over in the dim rays of her nightlight. His striped tabby markings. His fierce little teeth. The white spot on the tip of his tail as he slapped it down on her comforter.

He was bigger again today. She knew it for sure. His little arms were muscular and his fur thicker. He was growing more and more every day, and she wasn't sure how she could explain it. She might have to ask Mom tomorrow if she remembered.

Still purring, Jynx started cleaning himself, and Julie let her eyes fall shut. She breathed in, smelling the fresh scent of the dryer sheets her mother used on her bedding, and then something else. It was the same harsh smell as yesterday, a smell Jynx had brought to bed. It was on him again, and she wished she knew what he got on himself so she could stop him from getting into it.

But there was more to that smell, and even as dreams called, and her thoughts became lighter and drifted, she knew that smell reminded her of another. It was similar, so similar to one she wanted to block out. It was there at the movies. It was just like the smell of that...

———◆◇◆———

When morning finally came, the house was cold and dim—or it felt that way, regardless of the temperature and lighting.

Mom was not herself. She sat at the kitchen table, drinking coffee and staring at her phone in a way that left the kitchen feeling drab, like Christmas had come and gone and they had just forgotten to take down the decorations.

Dad was in his room, working online. He didn't watch his Bigfoot shows. He just typed and clicked in silence.

When Julie came downstairs, Simon was on the couch, watching some show where people kept slamming into things by accident. A guy was trying to parkour over a railing and slipped, banging himself in his balls. Then a girl was on rollerblades and faceplanted into a glass wall.

Simon should have been laughing. He always laughed so loudly when he watched those shows. He wasn't, though.

Julie sat on the couch, a cushion away. She wanted to laugh too, but she didn't.

They didn't talk about the previous night. Neither of them wanted to think about it, let alone talk about it. The scene felt like it was still all around them, a haze in their minds as they sat silently in their living room. The giant beast was a cloud over the coffee table. The blood and gore were all over their floor. The smoke from Josh's gun hung in the air between them and the television. And they watched that screen through it all, ignoring it, pretending it wasn't there, holding back the reality of stress and despair that was clawing at their insides.

Mom's phone rang in the kitchen. She mumbled a few tired words and answered it.

"I don't know, Lisa. After last night... I know, but... Yeah, I get that. For a little while, okay."

Julie didn't turn until Mom came into the room a few minutes later and sat between her and her brother.

"Marcy wants you to come over." Mom's voice was careful. It wasn't how she usually talked. It was timid yet controlled, as if she might break something if she spoke too loudly. "She's doing crafts or something, and her mom said she would love to see you."

Julie looked at her mother skeptically. She was pretty sure Mom wanted to keep her and her brother at home on house arrest until the police captured whatever villain they thought was responsible for the movie theater bloodbath and the other disappearances.

"Is that okay?" Julie finally asked.

Mom sighed and reluctantly nodded. "I think Marcy's taking things pretty rough. If you're up to it, it would be a good thing to do as her friend."

"So I can go out?"

Mom's face went white. "No. Just to her house. From our front door to hers."

"Oh. No sledding."

"No."

It wasn't like she was in the mood for sledding, but Julie thought she had to ask—to know the rules.

"And I'm going to stand on the porch and watch you go over there."

"Really?"

"Yes. You better believe it." Mom turned to Simon. "What about you? Why don't you invite Tommy over?"

Julie knew Mom was really stretching there. She had a lot of problems with Tommy, especially his attitude, so to suggest that Simon invite him over was quite a gesture.

"He doesn't like coming here." Simon's eyes didn't leave his show.

She frowned. "Why?"

"We don't have any video games."

Mom sighed and nodded. "Fine. If you want to go to his house and play, you can. But same rules. There and back, and I'm watching."

To that, Simon turned. "Really?"

It took about half an hour for Simon to call Tommy and arrange things, Julie and her brother to get ready, and them both to venture to their friends' houses under their mother's watchful eye. It was so watchful that when Julie stepped inside the Burrows home and shut the door behind her, she could feel Mom's gaze fall away. It kind of felt cold, like stepping out of the sun and into a shadow, and she instantly missed her mother.

"In here." Ms. Burrows guided Julie into the kitchen. "Thank you so much for visiting us."

On the kitchen table, Marcy's jewelry-making kit was spread from one side to the other. Beads, wires, trinkets, thread, it was all there, anything a girl could have wanted to use to make herself a necklace or bracelet or earring. And Marcy was sitting there, staring at it all blankly, the same haze surrounding her that had taken over the Butler living room.

Julie didn't like that. She didn't like seeing her brother that way either, but there was something about seeing Marcy's free spirit sucked into the ether that ate a pit into the center of Julie's stomach.

She sat at the table beside her friend and picked up one of the needle-nose pliers and a piece of wire—she was nearly as adept at using the kit as Marcy was. She bent a loop at the end of the wire and threaded a few red beads onto it.

"What do you think about using Christmas colors?" Julie asked.

Marcy glanced at the beads, then her mother, then back into empty space.

"I haven't been able to get my mom a gift yet. I think she would like something Christmas colored."

Ms. Burrows bowed her head and left the room.

Julie heard her go, but for some reason, it wasn't the mother's movement that drew her gaze; it was the pottery sitting on top of the cabinets.

Three pieces seemed to gaze down at her. One was a large bowl trimmed with scratchy marks that didn't quite make sense to her. They made circles and stick shapes, crisscrossing each other like huge trees sprouting from a tiny planet. There was a tall one that almost looked like a vase only there were no flowers. It was trimmed with similar stick shapes and a rough drawing of a wolf. The third piece was too short for Julie to see completely. She only saw the upper edges of it and the handles of whatever was lying on top of it. The handles almost looked like bone.

"I think a Christmas theme would be nice," Marcy said. She picked up a few green beads and let them roll around on her cupped palm.

Julie was happy to hear Marcy's voice. "Do you think I should make a necklace or a bracelet?"

Marcy tilted her head, looking at the items on the table and contemplating. She picked up a trinket from the center and held it out for Julie to take. "A necklace. With this one in the middle."

Julie took the item and held it in her grip, where she could get a better look at it. It was a white stone, something like a pendant, with a hole at the top to dangle from. What was in the middle of the stone made Julie do a double-take between it and the pottery: a tiny carved drawing of a thin-lined shape, something like a tree but with more marks around it.

"What is this?" Julie asked. "It's kind of like those, isn't it? What are those?"

Marcy smiled at her friend. She got up and walked over to Julie and hugged her. "It's for good luck."

Julie hugged her back. She could tell that what her mom had said was true. Marcy was taking yesterday's event's pretty hard—especially since Ben was still missing as far as they knew.

"Thanks for coming, Julie." Marcy straightened up. Tears bulged from the corners of her eyes. "Please, finish your gift. I need to go lay down."

"You sure? I can come play in your room with you."

"Yeah." Marcy walked to the door and paused. She pointed at the pottery over the cabinet. "One day, we'll show you."

She went upstairs to bed. Julie finished her necklace and went home. She didn't see Marcy again for longer than she expected.

DECEMBER 21ST

4 Days 'til Christmas.

TOMMY HIGGINS'S ROOM WAS warmer than Simon's. That fact confronted him every winter day that he visited his friend's house. It wasn't that his own room was cold—his parents wouldn't let him freeze to death in his own house—but with the woodstove in the living room and the baseboard heaters usually set to low, his parents' attitude was more of the *just-put-on-a-sweater* variety when it came to turning up the heat. Tommy's mother was obviously more concerned with their comfort than their heating bill.

Simon thought there was something comforting in that—in being able to treat money that way. He hoped he could do that when he got older, not always feel like he had to scrimp and save like his parents. There was a part of him that, seeing the way Tommy lived, resented his parents for living the way they did—for forcing him to live that way. He tried not to feel angry and place blame, but sometimes it was hard, especially when he was sitting in Tommy's room, hoodie off, comfortable, playing video games his parents couldn't afford, and knowing they would soon go down to Tommy's kitchen, with a full cupboard, and eat whatever they wanted for lunch.

He buried those thoughts in the back of his mind as they took turns playing a fantasy game, passing the controller back and forth when they died or changed worlds, or when Tommy had a whim and just wanted the controller back. It was a nice distraction for both of them—a nice way for them to pretend the events at the movie theater hadn't happened and Robin and Ben Andrews weren't still missing and feared dead.

It was about one in the afternoon when their bag of cheese puffs went dry and they decided to take a break from the pixel world in search of something more substantial to eat.

Tommy's house was barely decorated for Christmas. It was a little strange to Simon, whose home was drenched from head to toe in something glittery, elf covered, or lit with LEDs. But where Tommy's house astounded Simon every year was the massive pile of presents under the tree, virtually overflowing like a sea from under its branches. Simon didn't stare, but he wanted to. He wanted to scope out each one and try to guess what was inside it. He was sure they weren't homemade crafts, second-hand toys, or school clothes.

They passed Tommy's mom on the couch on their way to the kitchen. She was watching some sort of fashion show and kept a tight grip on the wine glass in her hand. She didn't say anything to them until her show hit a commercial and they were through the threshold into the kitchen.

"You guys want me to make you something?" She dragged her Ss, and her voice was too loud for how far away they were.

Tommy shook his head where she couldn't see him and yelled back, "No, we got it." He glanced at Simon, obviously embarrassed, and made a drinking gesture with his thumb toward his mouth and tipping his hand up and back.

Simon shrugged. It was rare that his parents drank, but he didn't fault Tommy for what his mom did. He for sure didn't want to end up like his folks—living like them, being poor like them, being disabled like his dad or toxically positive like his mom—so he got it. He leaned on the counter as Tommy opened the fridge and perused the options.

"Frozen pizza?" Tommy pulled out an iced-over circular disc with a completely dream-world photo of a crispy-pepperoni-covered artisan pie glued to the plastic.

"Perfect." Simon gave a thumbs-up.

"Okay." Tommy looked at the directions. "Can you preheat to four-twenty-five?" As Simon went to the oven, Tommy set the pie on the counter and ripped open the plastic.

The stove was about twenty years newer than Simon's was, and he liked it a lot better. There were no cracked buttons, just a digital display. He tapped bake, used the up arrow to set the temperature, and tapped *start*.

Tommy pulled pepperonis off the frozen pizza, rearranging them from being glued on one side into a more even distribution.

Simon sat in one of the tall bar chairs that lined the other side of the counter and waited.

When Tommy was done and the oven was yet to be ready, they stood in awkward silence.

With nothing coming to mind to say other than the subject they were obviously both reliving in their minds, Simon finally broke their unstated rule to not speak about it. "So, do you think they'll find Robin and her brother?"

Tommy's face scrunched up. He looked mad for a moment, then he slouched into himself and said, "Man, I think they're both dead."

Neither Simon nor Tommy saw what had happened that night—not the full extent of it. They fled together into the closest theater; when the screaming had started and that thing burst into the lobby, it was pandemonium, every man for themselves. Simon felt a bit bad about that, that he couldn't and didn't try to help anyone else. But what could he have done?

"I thought that too." Simon shook his head. "But why haven't they found them?"

"Maybe it took them? Probably it ate them. The cops didn't find

Mr. Polson, remember? They were searching for him for days. Coach Cabbage? That monster..." He paused and took a breath. "That thing was crazy." He stared at the floor.

"It was bigger than a bear. I don't know how it even got in there."

"It was like a monster-cat." Tommy lifted his gaze, his melancholy seemingly broken by wonder. "Did you see the size of its paws? Of its head?"

"It was like something from a movie. I couldn't believe it at first." Simon nodded, happy to see his friend uplifted if only for a moment. "What do you think it was?"

"If this was a movie, it would have to be something mystical—a monster from another dimension. If I was to guess, though, I'd say a government experiment gone wrong. Some kind of messed-up DNA or cloning thing that went haywire. Like the Military Industrial Complex was messing with biological agents for the next war—if drones couldn't do the job for fear of EMPs or something, they could drop in these monsters to kill the other armies." It was almost like Tommy's normal self was talking. Then he faded back inside himself. "But who knows. That's just dumb talk."

The oven beeped, and Tommy picked up the pizza. Simon opened the door, and Tommy set it on the rack.

There was another silence, and Tommy's mom came in, dropped an empty bottle of wine into the trash, and winced when it landed with a shattering explosion.

"Don't touch that, baby. I'll fix the trash later." She kissed Tommy on the top of his head as he cowered away, then grabbed a new bottle from the cabinet's built-in wine rack. She hurried back into the living room as her show's commercials ended.

Tommy shook his head. Simon wasn't so jealous of Tommy's life at that moment, though he wished he knew the answer to where that monster came from.

Tommy didn't know what time it was when his dad's car pulled up in the driveway, but it had been dark outside for quite a while. He had made himself dinner, leaving Mom to sleep after she passed out on the couch, and he was pretty sure that if he could stay in his room for the rest of the night he wouldn't have to talk to his father.

The front door opened and slammed.

"Jesus Christ," Dad declared, probably after seeing Mom on the couch and knowing exactly what she had been doing all day long.

Tommy focused on his game. He shot another player and hid behind a building.

He wished Simon was still there so he had someone to talk to—or that Simon wasn't so poor and had a phone so they could talk—either way would have been better than nothing.

He killed another opponent, turned, and another player shot him. With his dead avatar on the screen, Tommy groaned and set the controller down. He was playing like crap, and he knew it. It was barely doing the job anyway—every time he blinked, his imagination went into overload, guessing what had happened to Robin.

He closed his eyes and rubbed them. He moved to the bed and stared at the ceiling.

Tommy would not let himself cry. He just wouldn't.

He saw that thing ripping the woman on the floor to shreds with its rear claws. It sliced into her like it was nothing. Had it done that to Robin?

He could see it pinning Robin to the floor and tearing into her, sliding claws down her front and slicing into her over and over. He saw Robin's blood running over the lobby carpet the way that woman's had.

She didn't deserve that. He didn't know exactly what happened or how it got her, but he knew it had. She wouldn't have been missing if it hadn't gotten her. If he were to guess, the police had to wait for DNA tests. They probably had to test what was left to know whose remains were whose.

He rubbed his burning eyes. He was not going to cry. He was not going to cry.

Tommy jumped as someone banged on his door. It was Dad; he was the only one who banged that loudly.

"Tom! Open up."

Tommy sighed and rose from the bed.

"Tom!" Dad banged again. The door shook inside its frame.

"Coming." Tommy unlocked the door and opened it.

Dad scanned him up and down, then took in the room. His eyes went to the TV and the controller on the floor. "You just been playing that stupid thing all day?"

"What?" Tommy turned. In the few moments since lying in bed and his mind driving him nuts about Robin, he had completely forgotten that he left it on. "Um, some."

"I was just downstairs. The kitchen's a mess. Your mother's drunk on the couch. And you're up here goofing off?"

"I just..."

"We've talked about this. When I'm not here, your job is to help around the house and keep Mom from overdoing it."

Tommy nodded. "Yeah."

"Do you think she overdid it?"

"Probably." He didn't know how he was supposed to stop a grown alcoholic woman from doing what she wanted, but yeah, Tommy would have guessed she overdid it.

"Fuck. Probably?" Dad turned away. "And you're not supposed to be playing that goddamn thing unless the house is clean… right?"

"Yeah, but Mom said—"

"Your drunken mother? Oh, I'm pretty sure you could get her to say whatever you wanted in that state."

"Dad—"

"Don't." He held up his hand. "Go clean the goddamn kitchen. I'll be down in a few minutes to check on you. Then we'll get Mom up and into bed." He waited a minute, gathering himself. "Got it?"

"Yeah." Tommy could now smell the perfume. He could see the light, red marks on his father's neck where lipstick had been rubbed off. He ground his teeth together and waited.

"Good." Tommy's father turned and went into his room, probably to shower off what his secretary had left on him.

Tommy wished he was five years older and fifty pounds heavier. He wished he could raise his fists and lay his father out on the hallway carpet outside his room and go on with his day. He assured himself that day would come, and he headed downstairs.

Mom's show was still streaming—loudly—on the television, and she was snoring on the couch. Tommy picked up her glass and the wine bottle on his way to the kitchen.

The kitchen wasn't that bad, but Dad was always in a crappy mood when he had to work on the weekends and even crappier still when Mom was drunk. But did he even bother to ask if she would be drinking so much if he was there with them instead of off with *her*?

He put the wine in the fridge and the glass in the dishwasher. He picked up the frozen pizza trash and the empty chip bags. He put the cups and plates he and Simon had used in the dishwasher and started it. There were three wine corks on the counter, and he tossed them into the garbage.

That was it. He was done with the *mess*. He just had to wait for Dad so they could move his mother into her bed.

Tommy headed toward the living room. He figured he could sit and watch TV until Dad was down.

The smell hit him before he reached the door to the living room. When he saw what was going on, he didn't know if he was imagining things again or if he had gone insane.

The thing—the bear-sized animal—was in his living room, and it was chewing on his mother's leg.

Fear ran over him like a cold rain. It soaked him and coated him from his head down to his toes, and his entire body ceased to function. He watched his mother shake as it gnawed on her knee—everything below that was gone other than a layer of blood that turned the couch from beige into a dark crimson. She groaned, but she didn't wake, and he wanted to cry. What he did was piss down his leg.

It only took seconds before her knee was gone and it had swallowed her thigh. The crunching sound of mangled bone grated on Tommy's ears, and when the monster stopped so it could switch and eat her other leg, Tommy finally empowered himself to move.

He hated himself for what he did. He was finally able to control his body, and what did he do? If someone had asked him three days ago what he would have done in this situation, he would have told them he would grab the biggest knife in the kitchen and charge at the thing. He would have said it would be him and the monster, face to face.

That wasn't what he did.

Tommy slipped past the door jamb into the kitchen, his knees so weak they barely held him up. Out of sight of the monster, he forced himself against the wall. Panic controlled his every move, and that panic said that if he made a sound, the monster would be on top of him like it had been on that woman in the lobby, like it was on top of Mom.

He breathed slowly, pressed against that wall, and slid down the slick, eggshell-painted drywall. As his rear reached the floor, he heard it again—the monster. It was chewing. It was chomping. It was crushing Mom's bones between its teeth as it fed, like an industrial grinder turning beef and bone into ground hamburger.

That was what it did to Robin, to Coach Cabbage, to Mr. Polson. He was sure.

He couldn't breathe. The bright kitchen in front of him went dim, and spots filled his vision. He thought maybe he was dying, too, and he wondered if he deserved it for not running in there with a knife and saving his mother like a good son should have.

Then something changed. It stopped chewing, and Tommy heard Dad scream, "What the fuck?"

Tommy wanted to turn and see. He wanted to help his dad. He wanted to do anything more than press himself against a wall and hide.

There was a bang and a thump. His father screamed, then gurgled.

The chewing noises returned, and Tommy's face became wet. He was crying. His family needed him, and all he could do was cringe and cry. He wanted to run in there and let it eat him out of shame, and he could not get his limbs to move to do that.

So he sat and he listened. He heard it all, and though he could not see what it was doing, he could picture it in his mind. And he knew he would never be free of it.

It ate slowly, and then the noises stopped. A lot of time passed after that before he had the courage to look into the living room. When he did, he found only a lake of blood, and he thought he deserved to be part of it.

Tommy called the police, but when the operator answered the call, he found he couldn't speak to tell them to come. They finally showed up, something about their policy to check out every call, and he couldn't answer their questions. It wasn't that he didn't understand them; it was something else, like his mind wouldn't let him say the words. He couldn't say *It was a monster*, or *Mom and Dad are dead*.

The lights brought the Butlers to see what was happening, and Tommy went with them to their house. Mrs. Butler said it would be like a sleepover and he could stay in Simon's room. He liked that idea. It was a sleepover, that was all.

DECEMBER 22ND

3 Days 'til Christmas.

JULIE FELL ASLEEP LATE after hearing what happened to Tommy's parents and then him coming over. On most days the boy annoyed her to no end, and because of that, she wasn't a big fan of Simon being best friends with him. But after what happened to his parents, she felt like she needed to reevaluate everything. He was just a kid. They were just regular people. None of them deserved what had happened. And maybe she was too hard on him.

While she may have gone to bed later than usual, Simon and Tommy seemed like they were up all night. It was like every hour or so something loud happened on the other side of Julie's bedroom wall. Then she was awake, looking for Jynx and cuddling him again as she fell back to sleep.

Either way, it was around eleven in the morning before she woke for the day and ventured out of bed. She might not have gotten up before noon after her constantly interrupted sleep, but Jynx kneading his paws on her face told her that it was time for his (late) breakfast.

"Okay, okay," she grumbled as she pulled back the sheets.

He meowed. It was cute, but with sleep in her eyes and more yawns than brainpower to drive her, she had to fight back a hard case of grumpy frustration.

She got up, and he jumped off the bed. Even with the carpet, he thudded onto the floor with the impact of a cat twice his girth. She might have noticed it if she wasn't so sleepy.

Julie opened her bedroom door, and Jynx sprinted to the stairs, where he paused and waited.

The hallway was finally quiet except for the reverberating soundtrack of the downstairs TV. Obviously, Simon and Tommy had finally fallen asleep and were in no rush to wake up. It was Monday, so Mom was at work, and Julie never knew what Dad was up to until she saw him. Depending on his nerves, he could have been in his chair, the only place he could get comfortable when the pain flared up, or he could have been in his room, trying to get work done at his Internet job. With the TV going, he was likely in his chair.

Meow.

She was going too slowly, apparently.

As soon as she touched the railing, he raced her to the bottom of the steps and vanished around the corner.

"Whoa! Hello." Dad's voice came up the stairs from the living room.

When Julie reached the bottom railing, she saw Dad leaning back in his chair—he was obviously having a bad day—and Jynx was perched on his chest, watching her closely.

"Julie, I think I have something of yours," Dad announced.

She had to smile. It made her happy to think Jynx was warming up to the family and not just her. "Come on, Jynxie." She gestured toward the kitchen as she continued that way.

"Uff," Dad groaned as Jynx jumped down and raced into the next room. "That cat weighs as much as a bowling ball."

"He does not. He's just a baby."

"Well, your *baby* needs a bath. Plan on getting that done today."

She wanted to roll her eyes, but she knew Dad was right. "Okay," was all she said, but she wasn't exactly sure how you even bathed a cat. She was going to have to figure that out.

Jynx was on the counter, circling near the containers of cat food like a hungry shark. Julie grabbed a can from the stack, and the meows ramped up. She pulled back the tab, and they grew louder.

"It's coming, it's coming." She grabbed a butter knife and a plate and dumped and scraped. Jynx's face was in the food before she was done.

She watched him, wondering how something could eat so much so fast. The thought gave her a bad feeling, especially combined with his smell and the fish-scented food. She didn't know what that feeling was, but she didn't like it.

Julie reached for the cabinet to find something for breakfast, and the doorbell rang.

⸻◈⸻

Marcy had spent yesterday in her room, avoiding her mother's requests and attempts to soothe her as much as possible. She knew Mom only wanted what was best, only wanted to help, but these feelings were things she didn't think should just be swatted away. They were deep and profound, and she had never felt anything like them.

There had been horror and tragedy in front of her. She should remember that feeling. It was a real thing.

There was loss. Ben and his sister were missing—probably dead—and she was sad about that. Sad for Ben and Robin, sad for their families, sad for herself for missing him.

And she was scared. She didn't know what was going to happen next. She didn't know if she was safe, if anyone in her life was safe: Mom, Julie, her family, anyone.

It was a lot to take in and a lot to think about, and after what happened, she didn't know if she would ever be the same. How could she be?

With those thoughts accepted and settling deep inside her, she came out of her room today. Mom was waiting for her with bowls filled and candles lit. The scent of incense in the house that Julie always thought was from cigarettes was thick, and it made Marcy feel welcome as she sat at the table with her mother and took the knife in her hand.

"Are you ready?" Mom asked. There was kindness in Mom's face, but seriousness too. This was serious business, even if the reason for Mom's concern was personal.

Marcy nodded.

"You sure? There's no going back. This is early, even for our family. I didn't take the trial until I was eleven."

"I'm sure." There was already no going back for Marcy. After what she had seen and what she had felt, she was lost. She was in a world with no guardrails, where anyone could be taken at any time, and she was helpless to stop it. She needed something to hold onto, to feel like she at least had a chance when the world went all topsy-turvy upside down. She needed her mother to understand and back her up. "I'm ready."

Mom opened a box sitting on the floor, pulling a black rabbit up and setting it onto the sacred dish. It looked worried when she lifted it up, but it settled and lay still as soon as Mom released it. Its eyes were open, though it looked asleep.

"You know what to do," Mom told her. She sat straight up and closed her eyes. She placed her hands in her lap and began the chant.

Marcy knew she wouldn't like this part. She had never killed anything in her life larger than a fly, but it was part of the trial, and its life was being sacrificed for a reason. In the end, it was for the best if Marcy followed the right path and followed in her mother's footsteps. She had to believe that.

She tightened her grip on the knife, and her fingers shook. She braced them with her other hand and took a breath. She could do this. She leaned in with the blade and held it over the rabbit's chest.

Marcy studied the rabbit as she lowered the knife, placing the blade over its neck. She felt its body move ever so slightly as air filled its lungs and flowed out. She felt its heart thudding so fast inside its chest. She could feel its life, the heat that made it animate and function on this plane, and she wished there was another way.

But there wasn't.

"I'm sorry," she whispered, and plunged the tip into the rabbit's neck.

It shifted as blood leaked over her fingers and onto the dish. The blood was hot, warmer than she expected, and as she saw the animal still, she hated this.

Blood circled the dish, running over sage and roots and the rest of the mixture Mom had prepared.

Marcy laid her hand on the rabbit, hoping to provide some comfort to the thing as its blood drained. When she felt nothing left inside—no movement, no warmth, no life—she raised her hand and dipped two fingers in the bloody concoction that circled the plate. She said the words she had practiced as she wiped it on her forehead and cheeks.

She didn't know how long it would take the trial to begin. She was shocked when it grabbed her and yanked her away.

◆◇◆

Snow fell all around her from an orange, cloud-covered sky, and Marcy shivered as flakes patted on her nose and cheeks. She was wearing layers of fur and standing in an unknown place. There were trees, tall and pointed like the spruce trees near home, but she got the feeling she was not in Montana. Tall stone structures were scattered throughout the forest, some looking like boulders and some like stacked stone ruins, all from a time too ancient and too strange to have been built by men. She stood in the center of a thirty-foot-wide circle, and below her feet, a sharp pool of shattered bones poked up through the snow.

She didn't know what was coming. Mom couldn't tell her what the trial consisted of. But as she saw the bone floor and a line of rocks forming the border between the ground here and the rest of the forest, she thought she understood.

She had to stay within the ring.

There was rustling around Marcy, and the sky dimmed. Night fell like someone had thrown a switch, and the tops of the trees around the ring burst into flames. They were giant torches, lighting the area as things moved from behind and below the boulders.

Marcy straightened herself upright. Visions flooded her mind of the monster from the movies: the size of it, the smell, the blood on the floor. She ran her fingers over her hips and her legs, wondering if she had anything in her pockets she could protect herself with.

From every angle around her, things approached the ring. They were shadowed and hard to see, even with the firelight falling from above. They were fur covered, their eyes shining in the shadows, and as they neared, they grew from crawling things to taller things, like some kind of half-human, half-animal creatures that wanted to cross into the ring and feast on her the way that monster had torn into that woman at the movies.

Nothing was in her clothes. She wore furs sewn into a coat, a long shirt, and a pair of coarse, leathery pants. Her shoes were like the moccasins she was taught the Indians wore. She decided she was in some prehistoric place with prehistoric clothes, and those things in the woods were just as likely to be prehistoric monsters as anything—and she had no way of defending herself.

The noise from their rustling steps and the crackling debris from under their feet made Marcy's hair stand on end.

"Hello?" She decided to greet them. Maybe she could befriend them instead of fighting them?

They didn't answer. They moved closer, and they stared.

She waited for them to cross the threshold of the circle, but when they reached it, they didn't. They stood there. Watching her. Examining her. Their eyes twinkled in the newborn night.

What were they waiting for? Were they deciding which parts of her would be the tastiest before they attacked and tried to eat her?

"What do you want?" she screamed at the ring of onlookers.

There was a whisper that was neither voice nor wind, and it seemed to bounce from one onlooker to another.

Marcy spun, trying to watch them all. There were so many, so many furred people with shining dots in their eyes. She didn't know if she could count them all. She definitely couldn't watch them all.

Her heart pounded, and each breath was cold and stinging on her throat.

She searched the ground. Maybe there was something she could use?

It was a graveyard of broken bones, pieces smashed to bits like someone was making mulch. Except, there were a few...

Marcy leaned in and snagged a chunk that was as big as her arm that the mulcher must have missed. It was pointed at one end where something had snapped it.

The bone wasn't much, but if she had to protect herself, she could thrust it or stab with it. Maybe?

A cracking noise broke over the woods behind her. It was louder than the pat of fresh falling flakes on the ground and louder than the rustling and shifting of the watchers. It was an enormous movement, like a tree had cracked in half to make room for something far too big for the forest to hold.

Marcy spun. The crowd on that side of the ring parted, and from the darkness beyond the burning trees' light, something big approached.

It was massive, twice the size of the watchers. Its silhouette puffed and shrank with its steps like it was made from a cloud of pulsing fur. It shook the ground as it walked, and Marcy felt a chill that told her she was not the only one there who was scared of what was coming.

Thump, thump, thump, it came into the light, and her blood ran cold. It reached the edge of the ring, and her entire body trembled. The thing ahead, the monster stepping into the ring with her... it was *it*. It was the only monster she had seen in real life, the only thing she had ever really feared. It was large and black, with streaks of ruddy, red fur that was matted around its mouth from layers of blood, and that smell, the smell she would never forget; it was real, and it was right in front of her, and she wished she had never decided to do the trial.

She turned. She saw the edge of the ring, the one opposite the monster, the side she wasn't supposed to cross, and the creatures standing there were stepping aside, making a gap she could use to escape.

Thump, thump, thump. It was in the ring and moving toward her. Its smell was climbing sharply into her nose. Its size was twice what she saw at the theater. Its saucer-sized eyes were fixed on her, and she knew it was tasting her inside its mind.

It walked like a normal cat, though a thousand times as tall. Then it stalked like a cat, dropping its head and creeping lower, dropping its tail as the limb swooshed back and forth, slowly and deliberately.

The sounds the monster made were like screams in Marcy's ears: the crunch of bones under its gargantuan paws, the whoosh of air as its tail whipped, and a slow nasal hiss as it looked her over and decided what it wanted.

She was nothing but a mouse in this cat's playpen. She was a morsel for it to leap on and gobble up. What was she thinking? Doing the trial now? So young? She wasn't ready. She was going to get herself killed.

Marcy spun and ran. He feet crunched snow and dug into the layers of bone, pushing her forward across the testing ground to the ring's edge, maybe ten feet away.

She heard the monster move. There was a gravelly shift, like the pool of bones below them crackling under its feet. She heard the thump of its paces start and then quicken.

It was running too. It was running after her to catch her before she escaped.

Five feet left. The fur of her clothes whispered as she moved. She focused on the exit. She was practically there. The cold air raced in and out of her lungs. She pumped her legs so hard, so painfully; she strained to make them move.

She had to make it to that boundary. She had to live. She might have failed the trial, but she would be alive.

But alive for what?

Her mind ran through the emotions of the last two days: the fear, the sorrow, the helplessness—helplessness like right at that moment.

That was what she was trying to stop. She was trying to do something new. She was trying to live beyond those emotions that felt like crippling chains and make her life better.

If she let the same fear chase her from the ring, she was not conquering it. She was not learning to be stronger. She was the same weak girl who hid in that bathroom with the stall door closed, covering her eyes and her ears as her friends were murdered.

She couldn't do that. She had to be stronger. She had to be better. And if she couldn't, maybe death was deserved.

She had made it to the edge. She was about to step past it, to cross the line and fail.

Marcy stopped. She heard the thunder of the thing that was coming, yet she stopped. She turned back, her hand wrapped tightly around the bone, and she looked up into the oncoming monster that was bound to take her.

It leaped. Its claws were wide and extended and coming down toward her.

She raised the bone in front of her. If it was going to claw her, she was going to stab it in the chest. It might not do much, but that was what she was going to do.

She screamed. It was a howl like nothing she had ever created.

The monster came down.

She could smell its stench as its paws descended on her.

She readied herself for the pain and jerked her bone upward.

Claws fell on her shoulders, claws that should have torn her into a thousand slices, but instead, they faded into nothing. Her bone went up, and for the briefest of seconds, she felt it touch the creature, felt its fur brush across the back of her hand.

Then it was gone.

She blinked, and that place was gone.

She was at home, at the table, and the smile across her mother's face was one filled with pride.

She had done it, and she was not the same person.

A few hours later, within a confidence she wore like armor, she crossed her yard and knocked on Julie's door and asked her to play.

December 23rd

2 Days 'til Christmas.

Harvey and Lee didn't believe in going to bed early. They believed in staying up late and breaking the rules—especially on vacation. So when Lee was allowed to spend the night at Harvey's house and after Harvey's parents went to bed and told them to do the same, their alternate plan, which was too good to resist, just had to be done—no matter how dumb it might have been.

They went slowly, dressing in their snow pants and winter boots and sneaking out through the back door. They crept quietly around the house to the sidewalk and stayed silent until they were a few houses away. Then Lee let out a howl like a horny wolf that made both boys scream with laughter as they climbed the hill toward Railroad.

"Man, I can't wait to see what's in there," Harvey said.

"I bet it's like walking through a fancy store," Lee agreed.

Harvey looked up and down the intersection as they crossed Railroad and continued down the avenue. He saw no one, just a frigid night. "Man, it's like the town's abandoned."

"Even better for us."

"Hell, yeah."

But it was more than that, and Harvey felt it. It wasn't something he would have ever said to Lee, but it was fear, and he had it too. Fear hung over the town like a dense fog. It was thick in the air, so thick no one wanted any part of it—they wanted to hide inside their homes and hope the wind would blow it away.

But Harvey's fear wasn't from the supposed killer on the loose. He and Lee had gone over that a hundred times, and they just didn't believe in it. The idea that someone was running around a small town like Custer Falls and killing people—like a serial killer—was just dumb. It was another of those viral social media things or something, and even if the cops could get the entire town to buy into it, that didn't mean it was true.

Harvey and Lee were too smart to fall for that.

What Harvey was afraid of was getting caught. His parents told him that the next time he was caught by the police, they wouldn't hire a lawyer. Next time, they said they'd make him plead guilty and spend time in juvie. "Maybe that'll teach you to get your act together," Dad had said.

Still, though, even if they didn't fear the same things, he could still see it. It was like the air was thicker, and his face was cutting through it as he walked. It was like the scents of the night were tainted by something other than the smoke from wood-burning stoves, something that made a smell that all animals were programmed to flee from—including humans.

Yet Harvey felt like they were walking toward it.

"Look." Lee pointed at the house. All the lights were off except one deep inside the second floor that was barely visible. "No one's home, just like we thought."

A slimy feeling ran over Harvey's fingers, like he had touched something he shouldn't have and it might not come off.

"Man, maybe this is a bad idea." Harvey scanned the other houses, checking the windows to make sure no one was watching. "Maybe we shouldn't risk it."

"Risk what? No one's home. It's like Merry Christmas to us."

Harvey didn't know what to say. He wasn't about to admit he didn't want to get caught again, that he was afraid of going to juvie.

"Are you really going to pussy out?"

"Fuck no." Harvey punched Lee in the shoulder.

"Right." Lee punched him back.

"Let's go." Heart thudding, Harvey led the way across the lawn and onto Tommy Higgins's porch.

A yellow strand of caution tape still blocked the door, but Harvey reached below it and tried the knob. Surprisingly, it was locked. It relieved him for a second, but he immediately realized that a locked door only made things worse. It meant they would have to break something to get inside.

"Come on." He led Lee around the side of the house to the backyard, where he started searching. The flower bed along the fence was lined with potato-sized stones, and he grabbed one and took it to the window closest to the back door.

"Hell yeah," Lee whispered, "smash it."

But Harvey wasn't quite that dumb. He didn't want the noise. He took off his coat and held it against the window, then slammed the stone into that.

The glass shattered. It wasn't silent, but it was quieter than just tossing the rock through.

Harvey pushed the rest of the glass inside and pointed. "Go on. I made the hole, now you open the door."

"Okay." Lee walked over and climbed in. Lee could usually be counted on to take a dare. He dropped down inside and walked over to the back door, opening it and bowing like some sort of ritzy butler.

Harvey took one last look around, acknowledging how stupid he was. Then he went inside.

⬅◦➡

The house was warm, even beside the shattered window. Lee almost thought it was hot—was that how wealthy people lived?

He didn't know what had pulled Harvey's panties into a bunch, but he wasn't going to let it ruin this opportunity. He wasn't joking when he said it was Merry Christmas to them. They knew the Higginses were probably the wealthiest people in their shitty section of town, and Tommy was always flaunting his stuff. If no one was there—whatever the reason—it meant it was the time to see how the other half lived... and take a bit of it for themselves.

They crossed the kitchen, and Lee wondered if he should be looking for fancy silverware or anything; he always saw robbers taking that stuff in the movies. No, he decided, that was dumb—what would he do with thar?—but then he saw one of those fancy mixers on the counter.

"Look." Lee pointed. "Maybe we can pawn that for a few bucks."

"That's all you," Harvey said. "I'm looking for stuff I can use. I remember Tommy saying he had an Xbox."

"Yeah. Maybe on the way out."

They reached the door to the living room, and Lee had to stop to understand what he was looking at. He really wanted to turn on the lights to see better, but they couldn't take that chance.

It was like a black hole was covering the floor and parts of the couch. It was weird because in the rest of the room he could make out the carpet, like it was blinding white in the dim room—and where he was focusing, nothing.

Then he understood what it was, and it sent a shock wave down his spine. It was blood. The floor and the couch were so drenched in blood that in the darkness it was like a pit of pure black had eaten into the floor.

It made his stomach turn, and he didn't know if he wanted to run or puke.

"What's that smell?" Harvey asked from behind. "It's like something's rotten in here. Why'd you stop?"

He felt Harvey creep closer to his back, then look over his shoulder. "What is that?"

"I think you were right," Lee said. "I think we should go." The smell that Harvey had been talking about hit his nose. It was a repulsive smell that made the hair on the back of his neck stand up. It made him turn back toward the kitchen—not because he knew the source but because he knew that was the way out. "Come on." He gave Harvey a nudge back in the direction the had come from.

"Yeah." Harvey turned, and they each took a step toward the back door. They didn't talk about it, but they both felt it. Proceeding farther into that house would have been a grave mistake.

But the smell was heavier, and the dim moonlight that had been coming from the rear windows seemed to be blocked. Lee didn't know what could cause moonlight to go black like that. But he knew his heart was racing. He knew his lungs were panicking for more air than the house was giving him. He wanted to run, and he needed to do it immediately.

The next second, the moonlight came back, but not before Harvey was torn from Lee's side. It was like a flash, like Harvey disappeared into nothing, and the kitchen was lit once again with the pale lunar light that had shown them in.

"Harvey?" Lee hissed into the empty kitchen. "Where'd you go?" But he didn't expect an answer—not really.

There was a crunching sound, a wet crunching sound, and a weak whimper that made Lee shiver.

He acted in a flash. He didn't know if it was the right thing or not, but his instincts told him to do it.

Lee burst into a sprint and crossed the kitchen in a half second. He didn't risk going for the front door. That would have been too slow. He went for the window he had climbed through. He jumped when he was a few feet away, flinging himself into the air and through the gap like some idiot stuntman.

He was crossing the sill. He was doing it. Head, chest, and legs. He might have been acting dumb, but there was something in that house—he was sure of it. There was a pool of blood that something had made. His friend was missing, and he was scared Harvey might have been making his own pool of blood. Lee had no choice.

The night's freezing air was back on his face, and Lee couldn't wait to land in the cold snow, even if he was going to crash into it and have to run. He wanted to run. He needed to get out of there before whatever got Harvey got him.

He slammed into the Higgins's backyard and sprang up, planting his weight on his feet, and he immediately fell back into the snow, a snow that was—was it black?

And why couldn't he stand?

His heart leaped inside his chest. In the moonlight, the snow below him was indeed black—just like the floor, just like the end of his leg where his foot should have been.

His foot!

His foot was gone, and a stream of blood was gushing from his ankle.

He started to scream as he looked up. What he saw coming from the broken window sealed his throat and silenced him.

It was bigger than the window, but it slipped through like it was made of liquid, squeezing as it passed and plumping up on the other side. It was massive, bigger than anything alive should have been, and it was staring him down. It was chewing, chewing on something, and creeping right at him.

Lee found his voice to scream again, but it only lasted for a second. Just a single second.

◆◇◆

Adam Milton was frightened to his core. He knew he only had a few months left to live, but he wanted those months for himself. Yet there he was, putting his life in danger over something he didn't even know if he could change. But nothing would change if he didn't try.

The cat's bloodbath was ongoing, and even with Christmas Eve a day away, the blood would keep flowing. The animal was getting hungrier as the end of its reign neared. The screams from last night reinforced it. The thing was breaking its own rules as its time ran out, not just seeking out the ones who were evil to children but anyone who crossed its path.

He told himself he was doing what he had to as he held the plate of store-bought cookies in one hand and pressed the doorbell with the other. He had to do it.

The girl, Julie, he thought her name was, answered the door. She looked at him curiously.

There was a man asleep in a recliner by the TV and another neighbor child (Marcy?) on the couch. Marcy wore a charm around her neck that looked familiar and made him feel somehow safer.

Then he saw the cat. It wasn't a grown cat, but it was nearly there. It sat on the steps and looked at him as curiously as Julie, and that look sent ice through his veins.

"Can I help you?" Julie asked.

Adam realized he was trembling, staring at the cat, and he didn't know how long he had been doing that. "Yes." He lowered the plate of cookies so she could see the contents clearly. "I wanted to..." The cat was watching him so closely. It lay on the step, making itself more comfortable as it stared. "...to wish you a Merry Christmas. I was hoping we could talk for a few minutes."

Julie's gaze went from the cookies to Adam's eyes to her sleeping father in the chair. "Um—"

"It will only take a minute. Maybe we can sit in your kitchen? Have a cookie?"

He could see Julie weighing her options, nervous about the strange neighbor and waking her father. Adam didn't know the father's condition but thought he had heard at one point that the man was disabled.

"We don't have to wake your dad. Can we just talk for a few minutes?"

Julie, obviously unsure of what to do, glanced at her friend for help. Marcy looked Adam up and down, pausing on the trinket hanging from his neck—the old thing Amma had given him and he had stuck in a drawer and forgotten about sometime in high school—until now.

Marcy nodded.

"I—I guess," Julie agreed, and stepped back from the door.

"Wonderful." He handed her the plate, walked inside, and shut the door behind him—quietly. He was happy the father was asleep for the moment. He had a feeling that what he had to say would be more believable to children.

As Adam walked to the kitchen, he embraced the aromas of cinnamon and pine, the wonderful Christmas scents he had not filled his home with since childhood. He filled his lungs and felt his throat tickle and his lungs rattle. He settled himself—no coughing fits right now, they made others uncomfortable and he needed them to be comfortable.

He sat at the kitchen table. Julie set the cookies in the middle and sat across from him, still looking at him skeptically.

Adam peeled back the plastic wrap he had placed over the chocolate chip delicacies and picked one up. He didn't want one, but he took a bite and smiled to convince them it was all right, and she took one of her own.

Marcy joined them at the table, and Adam cleared his throat.

He wasn't sure how to start the conversation without getting thrown out as a crazy person, so he just started. "You got a new cat, right?"

Julie nodded and couldn't stop herself from grinning at the thought—she obviously loved the thing. "I did. He was a Christmas gift from my parents." That was going to make it harder.

"Have you noticed anything strange about him since you got him?"

"Strange? What do you mean?" Her smile vanished. She looked at him with a scowl.

He had to approach this carefully. "Has he been *growing*—getting very big very fast? Has he *smelled* at all strangely? Has he *disappeared* for large chunks of time at night?"

The girls turned to each other, sharing confused glances.

"What are you getting at?" Marcy asked.

"Did he do something to bother you? Get out and chase a squirrel at your house?" Julie said.

Adam could tell she was losing patience with him. "No, nothing like that." He got a better look at the pendant on Marcy's neck. It actually looked like a variation of the one his amma had given him. He reached up and stroked his own. "You know these tragedies and disappearances we've seen in town lately?"

There were footsteps by the kitchen entrance. The boys were there, including the one who lived next to Adam. They each grabbed a cookie.

"What's going on?" Tommy said.

Adam faced him. "I'm very sorry for your loss, young man."

"What about the tragedies?" Marcy asked. "What do you know?"

He took a deep breath. It was time to dive in. Either they would believe him or not.

"The thing that's been menacing the town—I faced it when I was a child. It's known as the Yule Cat back where my family is from."

Tommy's face went blank. "You've *faced* it? What does that mean?"

"It killed my parents." Adam felt his throat tickle. The air in his lungs rolled around like cars hitting roadblocks. He could only hold it back so much longer. "No one knows why the cat comes, only it comes and is gone after Christmas. It starts by seeking those who are evil toward children, but by the time Christmas approaches, it becomes gluttonous, so hungry and driven that it will take anyone who gets in its path."

"You're saying my parents were evil?" Tommy's face was bright red. "That Robin was evil?"

"No, I'm saying it's *hungry* now. When it shows, it will take anyone who draws its attention."

"Fuck off, old man." Tommy turned and stormed out of the kitchen. "Come on, Simon."

Simon turned.

"Please," Adam cautioned. The cat strode into the kitchen, and he couldn't stop a cough from slipping from his throat. "Be careful."

Simon left, and the cat stood in the doorway, staring at Adam. The coughing came in a burst. It took him hard and made him brace himself on the table.

The girls watched and winced uncomfortably.

He sucked in air. "It's fine. And I'm not contagious." He regained his composure, but he could tell a bigger fit was on the way, one he would not be able to hold back.

"Why were you asking about my cat?" Julie said.

He tried to say the words lightly, but he knew she would not take them well, no matter how he put it. And he was out of time. "He showed up at the same time this all started. He is constantly growing, constantly hungry, I'm sure. He disappears when the Yule Cat comes."

Marcy caught on. "Are you saying her cat is the killer?"

"Not exactly—but in some ways." He pointed. "The killer lives inside that cat. It comes out at night and does its deeds, then it retreats inside him. And there is no way to stop it."

Julie stood up. Adam could tell she was nervous doing so. "I would like you to leave, please." Her voice was polite yet firm. She must have learned that from her mother.

The cough burst from Adam's mouth. He could taste the blood and the acidic sting. His vision blurred, but he forced himself to stand.

The girls gazed at each other. They wanted to help despite the awkward situation. They couldn't.

He started toward the door, coughing as he went. He had delivered his message. It was up to them to accept it. He reached the door, and a hand touched his arm.

Julie was almost in tears, her eyes glossy. "I'm sorry. Are you okay?"

"As good as can be expected." Adam opened the door and stepped into the cold. His throat burned, and a steady wave of coughing continued. He paused outside the door and turned to the girl. He had to do more, even if it only gave them a slightly better chance. He took the trinket hanging around his neck and lifted it, pulling the entire necklace up and over his head.

He handed it to her. "This will not keep it away, but it may give you a some needed luck."

She took the thing reluctantly, not wanting to but feeling obliged.

He crossed the street, coughing harder. He made it into his house and shut the door before the fit drove him to his knees, then the ground, and he passed out on the entryway floor.

<hr>

Julie and Marcy didn't talk about the old man other than saying how crazy the whole story was. When Julie thought about the accusation that her little boy was somehow a monster, it just made her so mad.

She put the necklace the old man gave her on the kitchen counter and didn't give it another thought. It was almost Christmas. It was time for happy thoughts and playing with friends, and that was what she would do.

DECEMBER 24TH

1 Day 'til Christmas.

WHEN JULIE WOKE UP on the morning of Christmas Eve, Jynx-ie was on her bed, curled up next to her, just where he was supposed to be. He was bigger again—she could see that without even touching him, and the smell, it had gotten strong. Still, the idea that her wonderful boy was somehow a monster? That was just absurd.

She ran her fingers over his head, and he purred like a motor. He rubbed his face into her hand and gently nibbled on her knuckles.

He was the happiest little guy, and he was hers.

◆◇◆

At four thirty in the afternoon, it was hard for Julie to believe Mom was home from work, but there she was, pulling into the driveway. It may have been Christmas Eve, but that didn't mean her boss was any nicer—there must not have been any customers in the store.

Julie grinned from ear to ear when she saw there were two people in the car: Mom and Grandma. She ran from the front door into the dimming afternoon light with no jacket and only her slippers on her feet.

Grandma turned and smiled at her, and Julie was a little taken aback that her grandmother didn't spread her arms and pull her in for a hug. Then she remembered what Mom had said, that Grandma's memory wasn't doing well and she may have to repeat things or explain things. But did her grandmother not even remember who she was?

"Grandma?" Julie asked. "It's great to see you."

The woman's face brightened as if a light bulb had been flipped on. "Julie! You're so big I didn't recognize you at first!"

Now, she opened her arms, and Julie went in. Julie wasn't sure what to think, but she hugged the woman deeply. "Merry Christmas, Grandma!"

Mom went to the trunk and popped it open. "Help your grandmother inside, okay?"

"Okay." Julie stepped to the side and took Grandma's arm to keep her steady. "Let's go inside where it's warm, Grandma."

"You don't have a jacket on, do you?" Grandma walked toward the steps, and Julie kept pace. "I guess your mother didn't teach you that skill."

"It's fine, Grandma. I was just so happy to see you." They started up the steps, holding tightly onto each other.

The streetlights flickered on, and Mom followed them into the house. The sun set behind the western mountains, and the stars begged to peek through.

Julie helped Grandma to a seat on the couch, and even after Mom shut the door, the house seemed to have gotten colder. It was like the woodstove wasn't working quite as hard as it should have been.

"Can't you afford to keep from freezing?" Grandma asked Mom.

Mom bit her tongue.

"I'll add a log." Julie stood and went to the stove.

"Should be your father's job," Grandma said, ignoring Dad, who was sleeping in his chair after taking a painkiller an hour earlier.

"It's fine, Grandma." Julie picked up a log and opened the stove's door. The flames were roaring. By the sight of the fire's wild tendrils, it should have been a hundred degrees in the living room.

She added her new log and closed the door. "That should help."

Mom went into the kitchen, turned on the oven, and unloaded her bags. Shouting descended from upstairs, then a few chuckles. Jynx came trotting down the steps and yawned as he looked around the room.

"Julie," Mom called, "go tell your brother to come down and say hi."

"Okay." She ran past Jynx, bending to scratch him on the head, and climbed halfway up the steps before screaming, "Simon! Come say hi to Grandma!"

"Huh?" Dad stirred in his chair. "What is it?"

"Coming!" Simon screamed back.

"Oh, Beverly," Dad said, spotting his mother-in-law. He shuffled in his seat and lowered the footrest. "How are you doing?"

Julie sat next to Jynx on the bottom step as the adults talked. She rubbed his head and scratched behind his ears, and he purred and stretched. She couldn't help but think he looked huge, maybe as big as some full-grown cats. His front and back legs were long and thick with developed muscles, and his back was firm, his sides bulging.

She flashed to a thought of the old man's visit yesterday, his crazy idea that her cat was evil and possessed or something. It was a ridiculous idea, but she couldn't ignore the size of her boy or the odor coming from him.

Simon raced down the incline, leaping over Jynx and running into the living room. He plopped on the couch and hugged his grandmother as she pulled away with a look on her face like she had been attacked.

He let go and grinned. "Hi, Grandma!"

"Oh, hi," she finally said. "You're so big. I didn't recognize you at first."

It was awkward, and it would continue to be so for the next hour and a half as Mom cooked, Dad fought to entertain his mother-in-law between her bouts of forgetfulness and rosy insults, and Julie fed her cat and tried to make sense of his seemingly magical growth. And during that time, the fire seemed to heat the home less and less. The twinkling lights Mom had strewn around the house dimmed. The smells of Christmas things weakened, and the smell of the cat only grew.

Julie helped Mom set the kitchen table, bringing in two extra folding chairs from the shed. She brought her gift for Mom and placed it where Mom was going to sit. They weren't supposed to share their single Christmas Eve present until after dinner, but Mom had worked so hard to get Christmas ready for them all; she always worked so hard for everyone else that Julie couldn't wait to share it.

Mom made Dad turn off his show and play her Christmas music playlist instead. They all gathered at the kitchen table: the four Butlers, the matriarch, and their guest from across the street, who had heard nothing from the police or Social Services about what his future might hold—they guessed it would be the new year before that happened. It would have been a postcard-worthy picture had someone pulled out a camera app and had the run-up to the day not been brimming with death. Even Tommy was almost smiling at the joy around the table.

"What's this?" Mom picked up the gift Julie had left beside her plate.

"Open it!" Julie demanded.

"It's not time for presents yet."

"Come on. Just one for you? You deserve it."

Mom looked at Dad.

Dad nodded. "She's the boss."

Mom checked with Simon.

He shrugged. "Open it."

Grandma didn't look up from her plate.

Mom opened the small wrapped box and lifted the gift up high for everyone to see. It was only a token of what Julie felt, a small thing, a tip of the iceberg of what Julie wanted to offer her mother, but she beamed as Mom smiled.

"It's so pretty," Mom said. "Did you make it?"

"Yes. Put it on," Julie insisted.

"Can we eat now?" Simon whined.

"Yes, go ahead." Mom opened the clasp and put on the necklace as the rest of the table dug in.

Julie looked at the pendant hanging from her mother's neck and found herself glancing at the counter, where she had put the old man's gift. She stood and went to it. She held it up and looked closer, amazed at the similarity to her mother's. She didn't know why—it felt like an automatic thing, like running her fingers through her hair—but she slid it on her neck while walking back to the table.

Serving dishes were passed around, and the boys and Grandma started eating.

Mom noticed the old man's gift. "It's like mine, isn't it?"

Julie clenched her teeth, unsure what to say that wouldn't ruin the moment. How could she explain that the neighbor thought her cat was a possessed killer? She winced when her broken tooth reminded her it was there, and the question faded away as a low growl shook the kitchen. The light over the table flickered and dimmed, as did the one by the sink and the strings of glowing Christmas bulbs strung throughout the house.

"Can't even pay your power bill, can you?" Grandma asked.

"Mom!" Mom chided Grandma.

"What was that?" Simon asked.

The room instantly drained of its heat. Shadows sprouted from the corners and spread across the floors.

Dad stood from the table. He flinched as his nerve pain flared. "What's going on here?"

The smell of wild musk and bloody meat drifted into the kitchen on a wave of cold humidity. It sent shivers through them all.

A heavy thud sounded from the floor somewhere upstairs.

"I know that smell." Tommy stood from his seat and backed away from the table. "It's here. The monster's here."

"There's no monster," Dad said. He stepped toward the living room, and Mom grabbed his hand.

"Scott, don't," Mom told him.

"I have to see what that was."

"We should go," Tommy said. He scanned the room and pointed at the door that led from the laundry nook into the backyard. "Now. Now, we need to go."

"Sit down, boy," Grandma snapped. "It's dinner time." She picked up a roll and sliced it open for butter. "Shouldn't let a meal go to waste just because they can't pay the electric."

Julie held the edge of the table in her grip. She was being confronted with a truth she did not want to accept. She recognized the smell too. She knew it was the same one from the movies, the same one from her beloved pet. The noise—the thudding upstairs—it was Jynx's steps, the same pattern but heavier.

The old man was right. Her cat was the monster, and the thudding of feet across the upstairs, heading from her room toward the stairs, said it was coming downstairs. It was coming to do what monsters do. God, would he eat them all? Kill them all? Would he spare her out of love? Or was he so hungry—like the old man said—that nothing would slow him down?

"I'm getting out of here." Without coat or shoes, Tommy went to the back door and unlocked it. He paused for a moment, looking at the rest of them. "Aren't you coming?"

Dad headed across the living room. "I need to see what's going on. Erica, call 911."

Mom went to the counter, picked up her phone, and tried to unlock it. "It's dead."

There was a thud on the top step.

Tommy shot out the back door.

"Scott, get back here!" Mom shouted.

The lights died, all but the faint Christmas strands. The shadows widened, spreading like vines from the corners. The Christmas tree was almost black, and shadowy tendrils flipped around its edges like the branches had come alive and wanted revenge for the tree being evicted from its home.

"Daddy, come back!" Julie joined her mother. "Mom, we need to leave. Tommy was right."

"We should leave," Simon agreed.

Steps, noisy, heavy, thunderous steps descended the stairs.

It was coming.

Only Julie and Simon knew what to expect, and other than Grandma, they all knew to be afraid. Fear, infecting them in pulses, waves carried by the monster's stench, charged at them as if warning them of what was to come.

But Mom wasn't moving. She was staring at Dad, scared for him as he inched toward the bottom of the stairs.

Simon wasn't moving. He was focused on what was coming down, too petrified to leave even after suggesting it.

Grandma ate her roll, smacking her lips and deciding what to grab next from the table.

"We have to go!" Julie grabbed Simon, pulling him from his chair. "Go, Simon!" She shoved him toward the back door.

"But go where?"

She pointed at the door. "Marcy's." She didn't know why she said it, but it was close and it was shelter. "Go to Marcy's. Call the police."

"Mom!" Julie grabbed her mother's shoulder, but her mother would not move. "Grandma?" She tried pulling Grandma from her chair, but

Grandma shrugged her off.

"Oh god," Dad shouted from the living room. He was standing almost at the bottom of the steps, and Jynx—the monster—was only a few stairs away.

He was huge. He was the monster from the movies, the size of a bear but shaped like her boy. He was black and muddy red. He was angry, and he was hungry. And Dad was in his way.

"Scott!" Mom screamed.

Julie saw it in her mother's eyes. Mom was going to tell him to run, but there was no time and no point.

Mom opened her mouth again.

The monster leaped over the banister.

Julie screamed. Mom screamed.

Jynx landed on Dad, his jaws wide, shoving the man flat against the floor with a crunch. He lowered his maw over Dad's and closed his jaws as if Julie's father's flesh was as soft as marshmallow. In an instant, the front of the man's head was no more. Only the lower jaw and a crescent-shaped piece of the back of his skull remained, and Jynx lifted his head, chewing, swallowing, and went back for more.

Mom shrieked.

Julie grabbed her and yanked her, pulling her so hard she smacked her chair, threatening to knock it over. "Come on!"

Mom wobbled but she moved. She took her mother by the shoulder and tugged as Julie had done to her, and Grandma slapped her away.

"Don't put your hands on me," the matriarch shouted.

The monster chewed, and Dad's blood pooled on the living room floor. It soaked into the carpet, stretching toward the tree and the presents below, and Julie swore the shadows spread blackness over the entire house.

Something was happening, something even more than her cat murdering her father. Something evil, bigger than this, was sprouting, and it got worse the more Jynx ate.

"Mom." Julie tugged on her mother.

Jynx looked up from her dead father. Blood ran over his mouth and down his fur. It dripped from his whiskers as he turned toward the kitchen and set his sights on them.

"Now!" She yanked on her mother, and her mother backed away from the table, feet shuffling, brokenhearted from the vision ahead and terrified of the monster cat slowly crossing the living room. One giant pace at a time. Heading toward her.

Julie saw what her mother saw. Jynx was walking their way, but it was slow—he was stalking them. She shouldn't run. But she had to keep moving.

A step at a time, smaller than the monster, but keeping her going, she backed up to the door. Mom didn't fight but she didn't hurry. She went as fast as Julie pulled, and she trembled.

Jynx's head entered the kitchen. Julie remembered him racing across the room and leaping onto the counter for his dinner. She had thought he was so cute. Now, she just prayed not to be that dinner.

She felt the snow on the bottom of her slipper, the cold biting at her arms. She heard the growl and saw Jynx's tail whip in the darkness. He was going to pounce. He was going to jump on Mom and drag her away, and if she wasn't quick, there would be nothing Julie could do but watch.

There was a bang on the table.

"Where's the gravy?" Grandma shouted. "You never make enough gravy!"

In a flash, Jynx jumped, no longer focused on Mom but aiming at the elderly woman.

Julie didn't want to see but couldn't look away in time. As she pulled Mom outside and shut the door, she saw the cat's face buried in her grandmother's stomach. Arms flailed and blood sprayed. The shadows deepened.

But Julie had to hold everything in for now. She had to get Mom to shelter.

December 25th

FOR HOURS, UNTIL MIDNIGHT and beyond, they huddled in the darkness of Marcy's basement. The lack of light, the lack of power, seemed to have spread across the neighborhood and who knew how much farther. It was like the Yule Cat had sucked the electricity, the light, and every other means of power from the world.

Phones didn't work, nothing with a battery worked. They couldn't call for help, and even if it was safe enough to travel outside, neither Julie's mom nor Marcy's mom thought the cars would start with the way that everything with batteries was just *dead*.

So they sat in the dim candlelight of Marcy's basement, Julie, Simon, Marcy, Mom, and Ms. Burrows. They were quiet, and they listened to the wind that had picked up from a breeze to a howling rush of polar air. With no heat and no fireplace or stove down there, they warmed themselves by sharing blankets. And Marcy's mom chanted something every so often.

They didn't know what happened to Tommy. Simon guessed he went home or just kept running. Julie hoped he went for the police. The parents gently warned that anyone out in that wind and cold for too long could easily die of exposure.

There were screams outside every once in a while. There was stomping that made Julie think of a giant walking by. There were noises of crashing and crunching that rose over the wind's howl and faded as if teasing what would happen if the cat found them.

Julie hated herself for all of it. If she hadn't been so greedy for a cat of her own, the past week's events might not have happened. She had hounded her parents for months, maybe even a year, dropping hints and wishing. If she had just been happy with what she had, not dreamed of more, the Yule Cat would not have come.

Every scream was a reminder that she was to blame.

The shadows of the Burrows's basement were deep black, lit faintly by the candles, and though Julie asked about it, Marcy's mom said they were safe. Julie wished she could believe that. She couldn't escape the feelings she had back in her kitchen of the darkness trying to get her, the sense that the world around her, not just her Jynxie, had soured and was hungry to take her.

Mom pulled her in close and tightened the blanket around her waist. She pulled Simon in on the other side and secured his warmth. She fought hard to hold back her tears, but Julie could tell the difference between the shivers of cold and the shivers of loss.

As Ms. Burrows started chanting again, Marcy joined her, and Julie prayed for her neighborhood to get through the night.

◆○◆

Tommy sat in the corner of his room, shivering in the dark under his comforter. He didn't remember his house ever being this cold. *He* didn't remember ever being this cold. Without power and heat, even wearing his coat and under his blanket, he didn't know if he would last until morning.

He wished all of it would end. He wished his house was back to normal and his mom was downstairs, giddy with wine and Christmas cheer and making him a big fat mug of cocoa. He wished Dad was home and patting him on the back, reminding him that a man didn't get scared and a man took care of his responsibilities. He wished his Xbox worked so he could take his mind off all of it.

But Dad wasn't coming. Mom wasn't coming. All that was left of them was the dried pool of blood in the living room.

And he couldn't be the man Dad told him to be. It wasn't in him, and he didn't know how to bring it about. He was just a scared kid, and he wished he knew what to do.

The wind vibrated the house as it raced by. The roof creaked and the windows rattled. The storm wanted in. The cold wanted to get inside and turn him into another frozen hunk of winter.

Another crunch and a crash. Another scream. Another gust of wind that covered it all.

Tommy was thankful when the wind covered it all.

But the wind faded, and the ground shook as something massive stalked near Tommy's house. They were the footfalls of a giant, and they boomed through the ground and through the house, and Tommy clutched his blanket close because the noise was too near. And it was getting closer.

A crash of broken wood and glass made Tommy's entire house jump. He jumped as well, and his room tilted toward the windows. It tipped, and he felt himself sliding across his floor. He grabbed at the carpet and had no hold. He grabbed at his bedside table, and it slid with him. His feet pressed against his bed, and the bed glided across the carpet. He moved together with his furniture until everything was piled against the outer wall of his room, and through the window, he saw the black eyes of the demon.

The thing had grown. It was almost as tall as his house, and it watched him with interest. It wanted to know if he was another tasty treat, and it smacked the side of the house to test.

Tommy screamed as his room tumbled down and crashed into the dining room below. Everything around him shattered. Wood and glass and sheetrock erupted in every direction, and the only reason he wasn't immediately impaled was the mattress he rode down on and his heavy layers of clothes, coat, and blanket.

A roar shook the wreckage, and the wind cut through like a wall of ice. The monster's paw smashed through the skeleton of two-by-fours with attached boards and siding that had been his home's outer wall, slamming it all aside and crashing into the house. And Tommy did the only thing that came to him: he sprang to his feet and ran.

He jumped over debris, his clothes, his toys, his poor, shattered Xbox, and darted through the open wall into the downstairs of his house.

The paw chased him as he ducked and turned and slipped into the kitchen. He felt like a mouse in some old cartoon, just waiting to be snatched up by claws.

He found himself where so much changed in his life. He was inches from the spot where he hid and closed his eyes and listened as that thing devoured his parents, and he hated himself—his cowardice. He saw the dried blood, scattered with snow and debris, and his body shook uncontrollably. With the paw coming toward him, he fell to his knees and wept.

Would he be better off just letting the monster have him? Maybe he could see Mom and Dad again that way?

He didn't know, and he didn't think he had it in him to keep running.

He reached for the stain, the only piece of them that was left, and he heard a horrible scream from outside.

Adam Milton had thought he was done. He was going to hide in his basement, knowing he had passed along what information he had. He even gave that little girl the only protection he had to hide himself from its view.

But the screams kept coming. The crashing and booming footfalls kept sounding. The monster was on the loose, and it just kept killing, and he didn't know how he could stand it.

From his basement, with the small fire in the stove and his heavy winter wear, he tried to hide out. The heat barely trickled from the fire, and the light was sapped into barely more than a candle, and he thought he could deal with it, that if he just buried his head in the sand until morning it would all go away and life would be normal again.

Then he heard the monster stop at the house next door.

No one was supposed to have been there. The Higgins' kid was supposed to have been across the street at his friend's place.

There was a roar and a crash and a scream.

He was home. The goddamn kid was home, and the monster was on to him.

Adam wanted to close his eyes and plug his ears. He wanted to just let whatever was going to happen, happen. He was no hero. He couldn't save the kid. The Yule Cat couldn't be killed.

There was another bang.

It was destroying the house to get to the kid.

There was nothing Adam could do. But he couldn't stop himself from doing what came next either.

Adam jerked open the door of the woodstove, and with his gloved hand, he seized the end of a burning log.

He instantly felt the heat. He heard the sizzle of synthetic fibers on his fingers and palm. He held back the urge to shout and pushed himself to run up the basement steps and across the living room. He flung open the front door, looked through the blowing snow at the front of his neighbor's house, and saw the monster at its largest.

It was no longer the bear-sized thing that had been in his house, investigating him, several days prior. It was bigger than an elephant, and it was smashing the Higgins' house, trying to snag someone inside.

Adam trembled from the cold around his chest and the heat in his hand, and he knew a cough was coming. He burned. His hand smoldered as he held that log, and with the cough getting nearer, he only had a second or two before the beast noticed him. He used that second to think.

Did he really want to do this? He had a chance to turn around and run if he took it. Did he think he could live with himself for whatever time he had left if he didn't try to save the kid?

He remembered his father's bloody hand reaching for his help all those years ago. He remembered the lake of blood on his parents' floor. He remembered all the years in between, where life never felt as full as it might have if he hadn't watched them die. He hoped no one else would have to go through that. And he knew he would be living the rest of his days in Hell if he didn't act at that very second.

Adam ran into the wind as snow bit into his cheeks. Freezing air filled his lungs and shook his phlegm and swollen tissue and cancerous bulges. He felt a coughing fit brewing, a big one that would likely drive him to the ground and halt him from doing anything at all—maybe even kill him if it happened in this weather.

He only had a moment.

Even through the roaring wind, he smelled the cat. The heavy musk was like a fog that pushed its way into him as he rushed closer and closer, until he was right next to the massive creature—right under it as it reached into the broken home, searching around for the boy.

Adam thanked the gods above that he made it that far without being seen, and he raised his burning log up under the cat.

The log's flames and red, smoldering coals spread aside the thick layers of fur. They singed and sparked and set fire to tufts of hair, fire that rose up the cat's front armpit and around its shoulder so fast that Adam had to question if he knew what he was doing—knew how mad it would get and how bad it would be for him.

An inhuman scream nearly broke Adam's eardrums.

The cat spun and locked its eyes on him. There was hate and contempt in those eyes, a hate that in any other circumstance may have been enough to kill a man on its own. But as the cat burned, it could only swipe at him once before leaping away while howling like a thousand cats merged into a single belt of painful cries.

The strike cut Adam through his gut and tossed him fifteen feet backward into his snowy lawn. He landed on his back as the coughing came.

It was as bad as he expected. He cringed, rolling on his side, cough after cough, his lungs swelling inside his chest and blood and mucus flying from his mouth and clogging his throat.

He couldn't stop. The pain in his stomach, the slices from the cat's claws—they exposed his insides, and he refused to look. He knew it was bad; it was deep inside or even through his muscles, and it was probably the worst pain in his life as each cough strained him and tore deeper into his belly. But he couldn't stop.

The night drew darker as each inhale gave him less and less oxygen. It was only a matter of seconds before he was out, and he welcomed it.

If this was how he was meant to go, he welcomed it. He just hoped—

The boy crept out of the wrecked home and approached. He was shaking and crying. He kneeled beside Adam.

If he could have talked, Adam would have said *run*. Instead, he lost consciousness, hoping the kid would know.

<hr />

Julie couldn't stop herself from looking. In that part of the basement, they had covered the windows, but when she heard those screams, close, loud screams, she had to know.

She saw Jynxie burning and the old man fall. She saw the cat in pain and running off, and she saw Tommy.

He was scared, he was freezing, and he was alone.

Tommy was not her favorite person, but he was a person and he was her brother's friend. As she saw him there, orphaned and freezing, she knew when Jynx came back he would be in mortal danger. She had no other choice but to help.

"We have to call him over here," Julie told the others.

Mom looked nervous, but she nodded. Simon, who had crept near and had been watching over her shoulder, agreed.

Marcy glanced at her mother, who was deep within her chanting, then pointed at the back door of the walkout basement.

The three kids ran out into the storm, and snow pelted them with each step. It clung to them like tiny, clawed hands, trying to build and hold them back, but they pushed on around the house toward the front yard.

Julie screamed from the corner of the house. "Tommy!"

He stood over the old man. He didn't look at her. Did he not hear?

The wind whipped by, and its cold cut deep.

She called again, "Tommy!" and the wind screamed with her.

She didn't want to go any farther. She felt at least a little protected standing by the corner of the home, and she didn't want to lose that. But if he couldn't hear her...

She stepped onto the lawn, looking up and down the street. The snow was so thick there was no way of knowing if Jynx was a house or a mile away. She had to be quick.

She took off across Marcy's lawn, with Marcy and Simon behind her. She reached the street and wanted to stop, even turn back to hide, but she kept going, across the street and into the old man's yard.

She put a hand on Tommy's arm, and Tommy spun with wild eyes.

"Come on!" she screamed over the wind. "Come hide with us!"

He stood there, saying nothing. He looked her up and down and then did the same to Simon and Marcy. His tears froze on his face.

"Come on," Julie told him, "before he comes back."

Tommy looked down at the old man, at the blood seeping into the snow. He didn't look like he was breathing.

"Tommy," Simon said, "come with us."

Tommy looked at his friend and nodded. "Okay."

The four of them looked up and down the street and started across. The wind blew hard, and the shadows under trees and around fences wiggled, vibrating to a frequency Julie could not hear. On the gusts from the north, the smell returned, and each of them knew what that meant.

"Run!" Julie screamed. Her heart beat louder and harder than ever. Her stomach grabbed her and warned her that life and death were on the line and she better not screw up.

They rushed into the street, all four within arm's reach of each other. Snow filled the gaps between them, making it hard to see each other and harder to see where they were going.

But they kept moving.

Past the street, they stepped into Marcy's yard one at a time. The smell was getting thicker, and the night felt darker and darker by the second. They were halfway across the lawn when the roar lifted over the wind and caused each of them to stop and turn toward the street.

Jynx stepped onto Marcy's lawn, one foot and then another. His head was low, and his eyes moved from one person to the next.

He was judging them. He was deciding who was better to chase and who was better to eat. He was a monster with only the race and death on his mind, and they were nothing but prey waiting to be taken.

Julie watched the Yule Cat closely and waved at her friends. "Keep going—*slowly*." If the giant really had her baby boy inside it, a fast-moving thing would only make it want to follow. They had to be careful, and each decision counted.

They backed away from the monster, but Julie didn't.

"Julie?" Simon hissed. "Come on."

She raised her hands toward the cat, seizing its attention. It stepped another foot on Marcy's yard and slowly raised the last one.

It was ten feet from her, but it was so tall that it towered above. Its eyes were glued to her, and she kept hers glued to it. She wanted the others to get away—the whole thing was her fault, after all—and she needed to know if this thing really had her baby boy inside it.

Jynx lowered his head toward her, and she didn't know if it was to sniff her or to eat her.

She was sweating. She was shaking. The voice in her head told her to run before he bit her in half, and she held still.

The cat was slow and cautious, and she watched the twitch in his right upper lip, a twitch she had seen a hundred times in her bed when he wanted his chin scratched, and she reached higher.

"I see you, my Jynxie. I see you." Her words were soft, and she held back her shakes.

Julie's hand rose, almost to where she could touch him, and she noticed something odd. While the shadows in the streets and the shadows on Marcy's property were both immensely black, the ones on Marcy's property didn't seem to wiggle. They didn't stretch along the ground in black vine-like strands the way they did in the street, the way they did in her house.

What did that mean?

He lowered his head nearly to her level, and he smelled so bad. The scent rocked her insides, reminding her of the wilderness inside him, reminding her of his primal nature. She wanted to hold her breath so she didn't have to smell it, but there was no way.

She felt under his thick coat and found the skin below, and she dug her nails in, scratching that big boy as if he was just a kitten on her lap. She ran her hands long and deep across his chin, caressing his fur. She purred at him with her tongue the way she did in bed, and he closed his eyes and let her scratch and scratch and scratch.

He was in there. Her sweet baby boy was in there, no matter how big and mean he was to everyone else in the world. Inside, it was Jynx.

"Julie!" A yell came from across the yard. She was so concentrated on what she was doing, and Jynx was so concentrated on her, that they both snapped upright and turned.

It was Marcy. She and her mother stood on the front steps of their house. They held candles up, and they were saying something Julie couldn't hear. Behind them, in the window, Mom watched. At the corners of the house stood Simon and Tommy, each with a candle in one hand and blocking it from the wind with the other.

What were they doing?

Jynx rose. He stood at his full height, nearly two stories tall, and he started toward the front door.

"Get inside!" Julie screamed. She hadn't spent the last few minutes distracting the cat just for them to step outside and get eaten. "Go!"

But they weren't going. He was walking toward the front porch, and they were just standing there. But something else was happening as well: their flames were growing.

At first, Julie thought it was just the wind making their candles flicker, but it was more than that. The flames were rising. They grew wider, and their flickers threw more and more light out into the yard. That light didn't seem to breach the edge of the property, but the snow brightened, the cat lit up, and the shadows across the curb and under the trees receded into the cracks and crevices they retreated to during the day.

"What are they doing?" Julie muttered.

Whatever it was, it made Jynx turn away. He squinted, lifting his giant paw, covering his eyes like he might when the sun was too bright—and it was bright. As the seconds passed, it was like Julie was witnessing a new dawn. It was like the sun was rising and the candles in their hands were the instruments.

"I can't believe it."

Jynx turned away, and if Julie was right, he was shrinking as he did it. Was there something in those lights that broke the spell? That made him think the night was over, and it was time for the Yule Cat to go on its way?

She had to believe so, but as he started walking from the house, she also worried that if he got away he might find someone else to kill. She couldn't let that happen.

Julie raised her hands toward him again and called, "Jynxie boy!" She made S sounds with her mouth. "Come here, my boy." She wiggled her fingers and prayed it would work—dangerous again, heart pounding again, but maybe—she had to try.

He saw her fingers, and with his face pointed away from the light, he extended his chin to her one more time.

She reached far and deep beneath his coat, and she scratched like it was the last time she would ever get to pet her little boy. She wept as she did it. She didn't know if it was from fear or loss or what, but she let the tears flow. She remembered her father, lost, her grandmother, lost, her neighbors, lost. She cried for them, and she pet her cat—and he shrank.

Steam rose from his coat, and his body shrank smaller and smaller the brighter the yard got and the more she rubbed. Before she knew it, she was leaning down to pet him. She was squatting. She was sitting in the snow, and he was crawling into her lap, blinking with heavy eyelids, and going to sleep.

He was no longer the giant, nor the bear, not even the oversized cat he had been before the night began. He was the size of an eight-week-old baby, the size he should have been all along, the color he should have been all along—he was just a kitten, a helpless, little kitten.

EPILOGUE

WITH THE YULE CAT banished and night returned to normal, they found Mr. Milton was badly wounded but he wasn't dead. They called the police, and after a quick ride in the ambulance and eight hours of surgery, he was saved—for the time being.

The police were there until long after the real sun rose over town and most of the residents of Custer Falls were knee-deep in ripped-up wrapping paper. They took what was left of Dad and Grandma to the morgue. They found a few other neighbors missing or in pieces, including poor Harvey and Lee. They asked a million questions, most of which had no answers—or no answers they would have believed. When they left the Butlers and the Burrowses alone, Julie, Marcy, Simon, Tommy, and the moms were finally able to talk.

It turned out that the Burrows' property was protected on its four corners. There was a series of charms Marcy's mom planted a long time ago to keep their home safe—and yes, it turned out, she was a witch of some sort, but a good one. Unfortunately, the Yule Cat was so strong that he was able to cross the boundary, but it did make him weaker.

The candles were charmed as well. It was some kind of thing that called on nature to protect itself by letting fire act like the sun. Julie didn't get it, but she was glad it worked. She thought that was what broke the Yule Cat's spell, but Ms. Burrows told her that that wasn't it.

It was love.

While the charms and the light made the Yule Cat weaker, on its own it couldn't have done more than drive the animal away. It may have preyed on the Yule Cat's hatred of sunlight, but it wasn't strong enough to exorcise it.

No. What had been strong enough to force the malevolent being out of that kitten was the love between that kitten and its person. Love made Jynx want to be with Julie, and love let Julie accept it, even with it being so big and scary and strong enough to slice her head clean from her body.

She cried when she heard that. Her little Jynx was in her arms, and she couldn't help but hold him to her heart and hug him dearly.

Of course, the others didn't get it. Simon and Tommy said they should kill the cat. They said there was too much of a chance that the Yule Cat could return, and killing it was the only way to be sure it would stay away. Mom, she just cried with Dad and Grandma gone—Julie didn't think Mom could even sleep with the thing that killed them in her house, even if it was possessed at the time.

Luckily, Ms. Burrows agreed to let Jynxie stay at her house. She was sure the evil was gone and didn't want to see another life lost. It was a hard choice for Julie to make, but ultimately, she had to. But at least he was just next door and she could see him and pet him and love him every day.

And he would love her back.

⚫

9 days after Christmas.

Although the snow was still fresh from the post-New Year's snowstorm, it wasn't that deep. It was easy enough for Marcy and her mother to place candles and draw sigils in their backyard. There were many runes to mark and many ingredients to spread before the Wolf Moon reached its zenith and the ritual was ready.

They worked in the dark, cold but deliberately, anticipating, imagining the power at their fingertips.

When the moon was in its position and the cat was placed where it belonged, when the members of Marcy's mother's tribe were ready in their circles across the globe, they said the words and they drew the blood.

Marcy thought about how much she had to learn and how much of the world was yet to open up for her, and she knew Julie would agree if she really understood.

And when Marcy's eyes glowed red with the power of the Yule Cat, and her mother praised her, and the words of dozens of witches around the world confirmed her place, Marcy grinned under the wide, white light of the Wolf.

She was ready for the hunger. Surely a human could do a better job controlling it than a cat.

ACKNOWLEDGEMENTS

The Christmas Cat From Hell was a lot of work, through long nights and weekends. It would not exist without the effort and kindness of many people. I thank you all and regret those I may have missed. This is just a token.

Christina Hitz — Thank you for sacrificing time together, encouraging me, and picking up all the pieces I missed through my absent-mindedness. Thank you for encouraging me and being there when I needed you.

My Kids — you guys are amazing and I am thankful for you every day.

My Editor: **Heather Ann Larson**, your keen eyes and attention to detail really helped to pull this book together. Thank you.

My Patreon members: Thank you for your support along this journey. It was a blast writing as you read. Special thanks to **Jay Bower, Jordan Triplett,** and **Justine Lownsbury**.

ABOUT THE AUTHOR

D.W. Hitz loves the outdoors and enjoys making it a background character in his work. He devours stories in all mediums. He enjoys writing in the genres of Horror, Supernatural/Paranormal Thriller, and Science Fiction/Fantasy. He aspires to tell stories that thrill the heart and stimulate the imagination.

When not writing, D.W. enjoys spending time with his family, hiking, camping, and playing with the dogs.

Stay up to date with D.W. by becoming a member at
patreon.com/dwhitz

WHAT'S NEXT?

Check out more horror by D.W. Hitz and Fedowar Press.

The Shadow Over Lone Wolf Lake by D.W. Hitz

Sometimes dead doesn't mean dead, and sometimes family is bound by more than blood.

After the death of his cantankerous grandmother, twelve-year-old Drew Kline and his family move into her house. It boasts a vast, fantastic forest, a broad and beautiful lake, and it also happens to be Drew's father's childhood home and the place where his young uncle disappeared twenty-five years ago.

The night of his arrival, in the crawlspace of his bedroom, Drew discovers a miniature human skull. It's a curiosity between him and his brother Dean, sparking a debate about whether the thing is real or some well-sculpted decoration. When he invites his friends to spend their last weekend of summer break exploring the property's woods and his uncle's clandestine fort, which contains a burial ground of pixie-size bodies, they inadvertently find themselves trapped in a land of the dead.

What follows forces Drew's father to relive the horrific mystery of his uncle's disappearance and reveals a long-held family secret that has cursed generations. If Drew and his friends want to return home, they'll have to survive in that strange land as they fight their way back, and his father will have to confront an evil that will only be satisfied with blood.

Garrets Lodge by D.W. Hitz

Something is stirring in the woods outside Custer Falls. A haunted place that's been waiting a very long time.

Wanda heads out on a hike with friends. Stevie and Honey flee into the woods from the cops. They all think the woods will be their salvation until they find the terrors at Garrets Lodge.

Our Trip Through Hell by D.W. Hitz

Missy was always forbidden from visiting the abandoned cemetery. She listened for most of her life, but now her father's tales of buried gold and family treasure are proving too tempting for her and her friends to resist.

On a cold November night, it becomes a portal to Hell. If they want to return, they'll have to fight for it.

Camp Slasher Lake: Volume 3

A tribute to the glorious slasher movies of the 1980s, Volume 3.

Featuring stories by Jonathan Maberry, Will Suffer, MJ Mars, Brian G. Berry, Megan Stockton, Jay Bower, Eric Butler, M Ennenbach, RJ Roles, Angel Van Atta, and D.W. Hitz

Bloodtooth by D.W. Hitz

After nightmares begin in the small town of Custer Falls, Montana, in 1992, it'll be thirty years before they end.

After Wes Henson and his friends' field trip to Bloodtooth Caverns, everything changes. All they did was stray off the path. They didn't expect to break their bones and discover an ancient relic. But once it's in Wes's hands, he's the one that has to put it back. Because when this evil is awake, no one's dreams are safe.

THANK YOU FOR READING

www.ingramcontent.com/pod-product-compliance
Lightning Source LLC
Chambersburg PA
CBHW071942190726
48293CB00004B/1307